YORK NO

General Editors: Professc
of Stirling) & Professor Suheil Bushrui (*American University of Beirut*)

Gerald Durrell

MY FAMILY AND OTHER ANIMALS

Notes by Hana Sambrook
MA, PH D (EDINBURGH)

LONGMAN
YORK PRESS

YORK PRESS
Immeuble Esseily, Place Riad Solh, Beirut

LONGMAN GROUP UK LIMITED
Longman House,
Burnt Mill,
Harlow,
Essex

© Librairie du Liban 1989

All rights reserved. No part of this publication may be reproduced, stored in a retrieval system, or transmitted in any form or by any means, electronic, mechanical, photocopying, recording, or otherwise, without the prior permission of the copyright owner.

First published 1990

ISBN 0-582-03826-X

Typeset by Boldface Typesetters, London EC1
Produced by Longman Group (FE) Ltd
Printed in Hong Kong

Contents

Part 1: Introduction   *page* 5
    The life of Gerald Durrell   5
    Man and nature   7
    A note on the text   9

Part 2: Summaries   10
    A general summary   10
    Detailed summaries   12

Part 3: Commentary   40
    Structure   40
    The theme of nature   43
    Style   45
    Characters   50

Part 4: Hints for study   59
    Studying the text   59
    Quotations   61
    Preparing for the examination   62
    Specimen questions   63
    Specimen answers   63

Part 5: Suggestions for further reading   67
The author of these notes   68

Part 1
Introduction

The life of Gerald Durrell

Gerald Malcolm Durrell was born in 1925 in Jamshedpur in Bihar State in India, the youngest in a family of four children. (The eldest of the four is the well-known novelist Lawrence Durrell.) Gerald's father worked in India as a civil engineer until his death in 1928. After his death the family returned to England, but in 1933 they went to live on the Continent, travelling for some time in France, Italy and Switzerland. During this period Gerald received some education from a variety of private tutors of different nationalities: not the conventional education of an English schoolboy. After a brief return to England, where the Durrells were thoroughly miserable in the seaside resort of Bournemouth, they left again, this time to settle on the Greek island of Corfu in the Ionian Sea.

It was during these happy years on Corfu that Gerald had the opportunity to develop the interest in zoology which has become his lifelong passion. He acquired a number of pets, some of them of a decidedly unusual sort, and his meticulous observation of animal life embraced all creatures large and small in the island countryside and the seas round it. His formal education still remained haphazard, entrusted as it was to a succession of eccentric tutors. (We may well wonder whether his great gift as a naturalist would have had the same chance to develop if he had been put through the treadmill of conventional education. In his later career he never seems to have shown any interest in pursuing his nature studies in an academic institution, preferring instead practical work with animals, collecting them or keeping them.)

The Durrells returned to England not long before the outbreak of the Second World War, which put an end to their wanderings. During the war Gerald Durrell worked in agricultural research and studied animal ecology, and in 1945 he joined the staff of Whipsnade Zoo in Bedfordshire as a student keeper.

Two years later he organised, and, with the help of a small legacy, financed out of his own pocket, his first animal-collecting expedition to the British Cameroons. This expedition, which furnished him with the material for his first book, *The Overloaded Ark* (1953), was followed by a second in 1948, again to the Cameroons, which Durrell described in *The Bafut Beagles* (1954). In 1949 he travelled to British Guiana (now Guyana), again to collect animals. Further expeditions followed, to Argentina and

Paraguay (1953-4), once more to the Cameroons (1957), Argentina again in 1958, Sierra Leone in 1965, Mexico in 1968, Australia in 1969, Mauritius in 1976 and 1977, Assam in 1978, Mexico in 1979, Madagascar in 1981. In 1951 he married Jacqueline Rasen who accompanied him on several of his expeditions. The marriage was dissolved in 1971, and in 1975 Durrell married again. His second wife, Lee, has accompanied him on later expeditions, and collaborated with him on his latest book, *Durrell in Russia*, published in 1986.

In addition to his animal-collecting expeditions he has written numerous travel books based on these expeditions, and broadcast and lectured on natural history. Over the years the list of his published works has grown more and more impressive. To select only a few from a long list of titles, *The Overloaded Ark* was followed in 1954 by *Three Singles to Adventure* with a South American background. After *The Bafut Beagles* and *The New Noah*, published in 1954 and 1955 respectively, came *The Drunken Forest* (1955) which tells of Durrell's adventures in Argentina and Paraguay, and in the next year he returned to his childhood on Corfu with *My Family and Other Animals*. *Encounters With Animals* came out in 1958, to be followed in 1960 by *A Zoo in My Luggage*, a tale of further adventures in the Cameroons. In 1961 he published three books: *The Whispering Land* (on Argentina and Paraguay), *Island Zoo* and *Look at Zoos*.

Since then the intervals between his books have been growing longer, possibly because of his increasing commitments to television and to other projects which he has initiated. Nevertheless he published several books dealing with these projects as well as with his more recent expeditions: *Menagerie Manor* (1964), *Two in the Bush* (1966), *Birds, Beasts and Relatives* (1969), *Catch Me a Colobus* (1972), *Beasts in My Belfry* (1973), *The Talking Parcel* (1974), *The Stationary Ark* (1976), *The Garden of the Gods* (1978 — with a Corfu background), *The Picnic and Suchlike Pandemonium* (1979), *The Mockery Bird* (1981), *The Amateur Naturalist* (1982), and, with Lee Durrell, *Durrell in Russia* (1986).

He first appeared on television in 1956, and his nature programmes with the exotic settings of his expeditions attracted large audiences. His TV programmes include 'Two in the Bush', 'Catch Me a Colobus', 'Animal People—Menagerie Manor', 'The Garden of the Gods', 'The Stationary Ark', 'The Ark on the Move', 'The Amateur Naturalist' series, 'Durrell in Russia', and, most recently, 'Ourselves and Other Animals'. As a glance at the list of his published books will show, several of his television programmes were followed by books drawing on the same material.

As his audiences grew, he became more and more interested not just in showing the strange wonders of the immense variety of the earth's creatures and in telling his book readers about them, but in helping to ensure that the rarer animals did not disappear off the face of the earth, to be preserved only in the archives of the BBC. In 1958 he founded the

Jersey Zoological Park at Les Augres Manor on the Island of Jersey (another island—perhaps the happy memories of Corfu played a part in his choice as much as the mild climate of the Channel Islands and their useful closeness to England). This Zoological Park is now the headquarters of other ventures close to Durrell's heart, the Jersey Wildlife Preservation Trust, set up in 1964, and the Wildlife Preservation Trust International (1972). Both aim to establish proper breeding colonies of those animal species which are threatened by extinction. In 1983 Durrell was awarded the Order of the British Empire (OBE) in recognition of the work he has done and is still doing to make people realise how precious the vast and varied animal life on this planet is, and to show them what steps can be taken to ensure that no more rare species cease to exist, victims of man's ignorant greed which destroys their habitats.

It is no accident that so many of Durrell's books feature the words 'Ark' and 'Zoo' in their titles. The story of Noah's Ark—how God ordered life on earth to be destroyed by flood because of man's sinful wickedness, and how he decided to save two of each species for breeding in the Ark which he commanded Noah to build—offers irresistible parallels with the wildlife preservation movements of today. As for zoos, they were Durrell's first patrons, commissioning him to search out and bring back rare specimens of animals, a task which eminently suited his taste for adventure and his passionate curiosity about animals, and about people too. These two words may be said to symbolise two quite different attitudes to man's environment—saving animals to let them live as they had always lived, and saving them for man, be it for his material profit or for his amusement—which will be briefly examined below.

Man and nature

The concern over the impact of man's activities on his environment, and over the profound and mostly irreversible effects of our view of nature as something put there by God for man's convenience, is a new phenomenon. This is not so much because of a new, refined sensibility in man as because of the enormous changes in the scope of human exploitation of nature, caused by technological advances made in the last 150 years. Because of the advances in medicine more and more people survive longer and longer, and they all demand to be fed, and so more areas of wild life come under cultivation. Vastly improved means of communication open more and more remote areas to exploration, swiftly followed by exploitation which is made easier by technological advances.

Man's cleverness of invention seems never to be matched by a full understanding of the consequences of his inventions. (Nuclear power—and Chernobyl—is the most convincing example of this time lag between the employment of a new technology and a full realisation of its effects.)

Even where technology does not threaten us with disasters of such terrifying proportions, improved methods of exploitation bring their own calamities, less dramatic perhaps, but alarming nevertheless. The overfishing of the fishing-grounds round Europe forces the fishing-fleets to move ever farther in search of fish, as far as the South Atlantic. The stripping of the forests of the world is creating 'dust bowls', areas so dry that nothing will grow there, because the forests that acted as water reservoirs are now gone.

All these phenomena are bringing about, however slowly, a change in man's attitude to nature, a questioning of the master-servant relationship which has been accepted for so long. The ecology movements worldwide, now entering the political arena with the formation of 'Green' parties in Germany, in Sweden and in Britain, for instance, represent a profound change in our view of what is acceptable in our treatment of nature.

The speed with which our attitudes have changed (and are changing still) may be noticed even in Durrell's delightful narrative in *My Family and Other Animals*. The reader, amused and entertained, may suddenly be pulled up sharp by the unwelcome intrusion of a tiny incident. Is it right that Gerry should kill and stuff a bat? We remember that bats are now an endangered species, protected by law almost too late. Should he remove a tortoise's egg to add to his collection? Collectors of birds' eggs are now fined quite heavily, in Britain at least. He robs a magpies' nest of two fledglings, and however entertaining his 'Magenpies' are, some readers may be made uneasy. It seems ungracious, pompous even, to worry about the ethics of a small boy's exploits, but the uneasiness persists. Readers of his other books, from *Three Singles to Adventure* onwards, may find themselves in a similar position: is it right to remove animals from their habitat to enrich the zoos?

Durrell's later activities, both at his zoo in Jersey and in his Wildlife Preservation Trust, demonstrate the apparent contradiction between these two areas that interest him (capturing wild animals and caging them in zoos while preserving them), and offer a justification. Man has simply gone too far in his abuse of nature. All over the world animals have lost their natural habitats, and rare species can only be saved by establishing breeding colonies in sanctuaries.

The role of zoos is changing as a result. From being just places where parents take their children for an exciting day out, zoos have become breeding establishments, trying in a very small way to repair some of the damage done by man to nature. Given that one living species, the human race, has by artificial means vastly increased its ability to destroy other species, then if by equally artificial means some of the threatened species can be preserved at all, and their chances of survival strengthened, let it be done. Gerald Durrell's descriptions of his pets make us laugh, but by making us acknowledge our affinities with these endearingly human, inquisitive, affectionate, dishonest, mocking creatures they also make us see them as our equals on this earth, equally entitled to a share of life. By this, as much as by his work on behalf of zoos and wildlife preservation, he has helped in today's efforts to redress the balance, up to now so unfairly tilted in man's favour.

A note on the text

My Family and Other Animals was first published in hardback by Rupert Hart-Davis, London, in 1956. The paperback edition, which has been used in the preparation of these Notes, was first published by Penguin Books in 1959, and has been reprinted many times since.

Part 2

Summaries
of MY FAMILY AND OTHER ANIMALS

A general summary

The Durrell family consists of Mrs Durrell, a widow, and her four children: Larry who wants to be a writer; Leslie who is only interested in firearms; Margo, preoccupied with fashion and her appearance; and the youngest boy, Gerry, who is the narrator of the book. Having lived for years in India, where all the children were born, they are miserably enduring a wet, cold English summer in the seaside resort of Bournemouth. Larry has the brilliant idea that they should follow the recommendation of a friend of his and go to live in Corfu, a Greek island in the Ionian Sea. So off to Corfu they all go, accompanied by their dog Roger.

On arrival they take rooms in a Swiss pension, but once Mrs Durrell has discovered the inadequacy of the pension's sanitary arrangements, she is determined to leave as soon as possible, and the hunt for a villa with a proper bathroom begins. The search seems hopeless until they meet Spiro, an English-speaking local taxi-driver who had spent a number of years in the United States of America, and who becomes their friend, counsellor and guardian angel. Spiro finds them a charming pink villa and organises their removal there.

Once settled in, all the members of the family feel free to pursue their own interests. For Gerry this means a thorough exploration of the garden and of the surrounding countryside. He soon learns to speak Greek and makes friends with all the peasants of the neighbourhood. His friends include Yani the shepherd, old Agathi who teaches him to sing Greek folk songs, and an extraordinary mute pedlar who carries a number of rose-beetles tied by lengths of cotton to his hand and makes them fly round and round his head to attract his young customers. From the Rose-beetle Man, Gerry buys first Achilles, an intelligent and entertaining tortoise who meets an early death in a well, and then a baby pigeon, Quasimodo, who turns out to be a female and abandons the Durrells for a handsome male pigeon.

Gerry's mother is worried that his education is being neglected, and so a tutor is found for him. This is George, Larry's friend, on whose recommendation they came to Corfu. With very few suitable books George tries to interest Gerry in mathematics, geography and history by introducing various animals into the lessons as much as possible. Some lessons even take place on the beach. Through George, Gerry meets Dr Theodore Stephanides, a charming, highly educated man whose interest in natural history matches Gerry's own, and who gives the boy much help and encouragement. The two meet regularly all winter to conduct scientific investigations and discuss their findings. Theodore becomes a close friend of the whole Durrell family.

Spring comes once more and Margo acquires an admirer, an insufferably conceited young Turk. Fortunately, an unsuccessful visit to the cinema puts an end to Margo's romance.

Mrs Durrell discovers with alarm that Larry has invited numerous friends to stay. As the house is too small to accommodate so many visitors, the only solution is to move to a bigger villa, this time a yellow one. The gardener's wife, Lugaretzia, who helps Mrs Durrell in the house, turns out to be a dreadful hypochondriac, forever discoursing on her imaginary ailments. Real illness comes to the house when Margo catches influenza after having joined in the Corfiots' worship of Saint Spiridion, the patron saint of Corfu, and kissed the saint's mummified feet which, unhygienically, had been kissed by hundreds of others before.

There is a constant stream of visitors as Larry's friends arrive and depart, each one more eccentric than the last. Mealtimes are lively occasions, full of talk and laughter.

Gerry finds much to amuse him in his investigations of the old garden wall. He discovers a mother scorpion carrying her babies on her back and takes her home, placing her for safety in a matchbox. Unfortunately, Larry picks it up to light his cigarette after lunch, and the enraged scorpion jumps on to his hand. Pandemonium follows, and as a result of this incident Gerry's education becomes once more a matter for concern. First he is sent to the Belgian consul to learn French, then a young man fresh from Oxford, Peter, arrives to teach him. A romantic attachment develops between Peter and Margo, and Gerry is once more free to follow his interests in natural history. He acquires a baby owl, called Ulysses. As summer advances, the family enjoys sea bathing in the cool of the night.

Gerry finds a group of small islands, and in order to be able to go there as often as he likes, he persuades his brother Leslie to build a small boat for him as a birthday present. The boat is ceremoniously christened on the morning of Gerry's birthday, and his birthday party takes place in the evening of the same day.

Gerry's best birthday present — apart from the boat — is a pair of puppies christened Widdle and Puke by Larry because of their total lack of toilet training.

At the end of the summer Peter has to leave, as Mrs Durrell does not approve of his attachment to Margo. Margo indulges in a dramatic display of grief which soon passes. As winter draws near, Leslie is given plenty of opportunities to satisfy his passion for shooting. Larry tries to shoot snipe, falls into a bog, and while recovering from his soaking with the help of large quantities of brandy, sets the floor of his room on fire.

When spring comes once more the family has to move again, this time to a smaller house to discourage a visit from Great-aunt Hermione, a most disagreeable old lady.

The new white villa offers Gerry many interesting subjects for nature study, especially the mantids and the geckos. He witnesses a great battle between a large mantid and a clever and tenacious gecko in which the gecko is victorious. In the garden Gerry finds two huge toads which the family will not accept as house pets, much to his disappointment.

Another tutor is found, a Mr Kralefsky, a tiny eccentric man with a passion for birds. He and Gerry get on very well, though Gerry's education does not advance much. Gerry has found two more pets, a pair of unruly and inquisitive magpies.

Mrs Durrell has also acquired a pet, Dodo, a Dandy Dinmont bitch. Dodo is a tiresome little creature, passionately attached to her owner. Because of her great devotion to Mrs Durrell, Dodo has to be included in a family outing to a lake surrounded by lilies.

On one of his rambles Gerry meets a charming convict who is serving a sentence for the murder of his wife. He gives Gerry a huge, bloodthirsty black gull, Alecko; the rest of the household are not very pleased.

An early Christmas party for all the friends of the family is held in September, and in spite of various incidents, mostly caused by the behaviour of Gerry's numerous strange domestic pets, the event is a huge success.

The happy times are coming to an end, though. Kralefsky tells Gerry's mother that he has taught the boy all he can, and that Gerry should now go back to England or to Switzerland to continue his studies. All the children protest but to no avail. All their belongings are packed, the animals caged or put on leash, and the family travel back to England. Not surprisingly, a Swiss passport official describes the Durrells as 'One travelling Circus and Staff'.

Detailed summaries

Motto to the book

A quotation from William Shakespeare's (1564–1616) comedy *As You Like It*, IV.i; the speaker, Jaques, is explaining his particular form of melancholy, a humorous sadness caused by the amused contemplation of what he sees in his travels.

NOTES AND GLOSSARY:
simples:　　　　ingredients

The Speech for the Defence

In this introductory chapter, named after the speech which the defending lawyer makes on behalf of the accused person in a court of law, Gerald Durrell does indeed defend his book in a most amusing manner for not being an account of the natural history of the island of Corfu which he had originally intended to write, and for the extraordinary (and highly entertaining) behaviour of himself, his two elder brothers Larry and Leslie, his sister Margo, and of their mother, and of all the people whom they met in Corfu. So many pleasant and amusing things happened to his family and friends in the course of the five years they spent on the island that the author has been forced to cut out a good many of them. There is therefore no real chronological order in the narration.

The second half of this brief chapter is an extended and wittily unconventional form of acknowledgments, thanking all the people who had contributed to the making of the book, providing the author with such good material by their eccentric behaviour. He ends by stressing that all he has to tell about the island and its inhabitants, however incredible, is absolutely true: Corfu really is like that.

NOTES AND GLOSSARY:

'Why, sometimes I've believed ... before breakfast.': the White Queen's famous reply to Alice's protest that 'one can't believe impossible things' in Lewis Carroll's (1832–98) *Alice Through the Looking-Glass* (1872). A suitable motto for a book which delights in the oddities of human and animal behaviour

Corfu: island in the Ionian Sea off the west coast of Greece, close to the Albanian border

***Encyclopaedia Britannica*:** a series of volumes giving information on all branches of knowledge. Though it has been repeatedly brought up to date, the 11th edition, published in 1908 in twenty-nine volumes, is regarded as a model for publications of this kind

puns: jokes based on a word having more than one meaning, or on similar-sounding words which have different meanings

the split infinitive: an infinitive which has an adverb between 'to' and the verb. Disapproved of by purists, it is now quite common in English

shoals: shallow part of the sea dangerous to ships

Nirvana: in Buddhism a calm, sinless state of mind, achieved by the renunciation of all passions

14 · Summaries

A lesser mortal: a person not possessing her remarkable qualities; the phrase is usually employed ironically
slapstick: any broad comedy with plenty of noisy and vigorous action

PART ONE

Motto to Part One

A quotation from John Dryden's (1631–1700) anti-Catholic comedy *The Spanish Friar* (1681).

The Migration

The Durrell family are at Bournemouth, a seaside resort on the south coast of England. Having returned from India they suffer miserably in a typical English summer, cold, windy and wet. Gerald has catarrh, his brother Leslie is suffering from an inflammation of both ears, his sister Margo has acne, and their mother has a bad cold as well as rheumatism. Only Larry is free from illness but is greatly irritated by the others' complaints which he feels are preventing him from getting on with his job of becoming a writer.

As usual, Larry initiates the action that will get them all out of their present misery. He suggests that they should sell their house in England and move to Corfu. As usual again he gets his way, and the family soon set off, each member taking along what he or she regards as essential: Margo her dresses, books on slimming and cures for acne; Leslie his firearms; Larry a large quantity of books; and their mother a number of cookery and gardening volumes. Gerald himself is taking books on natural history. After a long train journey a small ship brings them to Corfu. The chapter ends with the first of Durrell's joyful descriptions of Corfu.

NOTES AND GLOSSARY:
The Migration: there is humour in the very title of this chapter, the word 'migration' suggesting the removal of a large body of people from one country to another
unctuousness: offensive self-satisfaction; notice how Durrell draws his similes from the animal world. Larry's unctuousness is 'cat-like', recalling the fixed smug smile of a cat's mouth
rain-distorted window: rain streaming across the window blurs all one sees outside
cleft palate: a congenital malformation of the mouth which makes speech difficult

Rajputana:	a vast area in west central India; as the Durrells had been living in India it is natural that Mother should be interested in Indian cuisine
eucalyptus:	oil of eucalyptus is used in the treatment of colds
the Town Clerk:	official secretary and legal adviser of a town
travelled light:	travelled with little luggage
chrysalids:	pupae, insects in the intermediate stage of development between a larva and a fully grown insect
Switzerland like a Christmas cake:	the snow on the Alps looks like the white sugar icing on a Christmas cake
the heel of Italy:	the map of Italy looks like a riding-boot, with the toe pointing towards Albania and Greece
wake:	line of foamy water left by the passage of a ship
cape:	land running out to sea
cicadas:	insects which make a continuous loud chirping noise

Chapter 1: The Unsuspected Isle

The Durrells have arrived in Corfu, and they all pile into a horse-drawn cab. Roger the dog starts barking at some dogs in the street and soon there is a mob of about twenty-four loudly barking dogs following the cab. When the cab stops outside the pension in which Mrs Durrell has booked rooms, all the members of the family are fully occupied fighting their way through the crowd of dogs while carrying Roger. Once safely inside they rest before eating an excellent lunch. In the course of conversation it is discovered that the hotel's sanitary arrangements are unsatisfactory, and that used toilet paper is not thrown into the lavatory bowl, but put into a little box by its side. Margo who had innocently used this soiled paper is in hysterics, convinced that she has caught some dreadful disease. Mrs Durrell decides that a house with a proper bathroom must be found at once. The search seems hopeless until they meet Spiro, a taxi-driver who has lived in America and speaks good, if rather eccentric English. Spiro takes the family under his wing, and finds a pretty little pink villa on a hillside, which they all like.

NOTES AND GLOSSARY:

The Unsuspected Isle: a quotation from Robert Browning's (1812–89) dramatic poem *Pippa Passes*, Part II, expressing a longing for solitude in Greece: 'Some unsuspected isle in the far seas!/Some unsuspected isle in far-off seas!'

'six of one ... of the other': Margo is misquoting the proverb 'Six of one and half a dozen of the other', meaning that they are both equally bad

tumblers:	acrobats
'a scene from *Uncle Tom's Cabin*':	Larry is referring to the famous melodramatic scene in Harriet Beecher Stowe's (1811–96) anti-slavery novel in which the slave-owner sets his dogs on the mulatto slave girl Eliza who is escaping with her child across the frozen Ohio River
with considerable majestic graciousness:	a mocking reference to Larry's earlier efforts to impress the onlookers with the family's gracious behaviour
dicky:	false shirt front
communing with nature:	going to the lavatory
filigrees:	ornamental work of twisted gold and silver wire
die like flies:	die in great numbers
'whys donts yous':	one of Spiro's most endearing qualities is his use of English: he adds an 's' to most verbs and nouns
Dodge:	American make of car
Spiro:	short for Spiridion, the name of the patron saint of Corfu
prickly pears:	cactus-like plants with clusters of prickles and pear-shaped edible fruit

Chapter 2: The Strawberry-Pink Villa

The Durrells feel at home at once in the pink villa with its flower-filled garden. Spiro takes charge of all their affairs, arranges the move to the villa, does all the shopping and forces the customs officials to release all their luggage. He is by now a friend of them all, particularly of Mrs Durrell. Once the family has settled in, they all feel free to pursue their own interests. Margo sunbathes and flirts with the Greek peasant boys; Larry reads and writes in his room emerging only for meals; Leslie practises his shooting; Mrs Durrell cooks and gardens; and Gerry explores the garden with Roger.

For a boy as passionately interested in all aspects of nature as he is the garden offers many opportunities for close study of insects such as spiders, lacewing-flies, and earwigs. As he learns to speak Greek and makes friends with all the peasant families in the neighbourhood, his study includes humans as well. His observations are minute and precise, and are described here in a style which combines visual accuracy with a delight in the skilful use of language.

NOTES AND GLOSSARY:
bougainvillaea:	climbing plant with brightly coloured flowers
pinched:	painfully squeezed
burr:	prickly seed-case of some plants which sticks to clothes

Summaries · 17

'you only die once':	another of Margo's misquoted proverbs: it should be 'You only live once' (and therefore you should enjoy yourself as much as you can)
horny-handed:	with hands hardened by work
Christian Science:	a religious movement founded at Boston, Massachusetts, in 1879 by Mrs Mary Baker Eddy (1821–1910). It is based on the Bible, but distinguishes between the religious teaching of the New Testament and all later dogma. It includes a system of 'divine healing' for which it is best known
Indian Mutiny:	rebellion in parts of British India during 1857–9. It started as a mutiny of native Indian soldiers in the East India Company's army, but soon spread beyond. An important outcome of the Mutiny was the transfer of government from the Company to the British government
hornets:	large wasp-like insects with a painful and dangerous sting
Carpenter bees:	bees which make their nests in wood
hawk-moths:	heavy moths capable of hovering in the air
a good purchase:	a secure position from which to act
lacewing-flies:	also known as golden-eyes, insects with brilliant golden eyes and transparent wings
Lilliput:	the land of tiny people in Jonathan Swift's (1667–1745) famous satire *Gulliver's Travels*
earwig:	insect which was supposed to creep into people's ears, hence its name
full complement:	required number
side-saddle:	sitting sideways, with both legs on the same side of the horse's body
a child's transfer:	brightly coloured picture which can be transferred from the page on which it is sold to another piece of paper

Chapter 3: The Rose-Beetle Man

Gerry's days are very full, with the garden and the world beyond waiting to be explored in Roger's company. During his explorations Gerry makes the acquaintance of a great many country people: a cheerful mentally defective youth in a bowler hat; a fat old lady, Agathi, who teaches him to sing Greek peasant songs; Yani, the shepherd, who likes to give Gerry good advice on how to keep safe during his wanderings. The strangest acquaintance of all is the Rose-beetle Man, a mute pedlar of trinkets and pet animals who carries a number of rose-beetles tied to lengths of cotton thread in his hand, making them fly round and round his head so as to attract customers. Gerry first buys from him a little tortoise which he christens Achilles. When Achilles dies after falling into an old well, Gerry buys a baby pigeon, Quasimodo. The pigeon turns out to be a female, and leaves the Durrells for a male pigeon.

NOTES AND GLOSSARY:

barred with gold: the sun streams in through the slats of the shutters in horizontal bands of light
his stump: his short tail
swaddling clothes: tightly wrapped clothes for a baby
puffball: round white edible fungus which can grow to a large size
bowler hat: a stiff felt hat with a hard round crown and a narrow brim, formerly often worn by businessmen in England
spindle: pin used for twisting the thread in spinning
bobbin: spool for winding the yarn in spinning
Vangeliò: title of a Greek folk song
'the little English lord': the belief that all Englishmen are 'Milords', rich noblemen, is perhaps partly due to the custom of the English upper classes in the eighteenth and nineteenth centuries of sending their sons on a Grand Tour of the Continent to round off their education. Partly, of course, this belief is based on the great difference between people who have the money to travel for pleasure and those who spend their entire lives in their village, working very hard for very little money
'never . . . sleep beneath a cypress': the cypress tree seems to attract superstitions. It grows in churchyards, and was regarded by the Romans as a funeral tree, dedicated to Pluto, god of the underworld
ply me: supply me, give to me
cataract: condition which affects the lens of the eye, causing partial blindness. It can now be cured by a simple operation
hoopoe: large bird with a high crest of feathers
kingfisher: waterside bird with brilliant blue feathers
The pockets of this garment bulged: evidently the Rose-beetle Man was a pedlar, a wandering seller of toys and cheap ornaments. His rose-beetles were a form of advertising to attract his young customers
a riot of handkerchiefs: a number of handkerchiefs of different bright colours

Summaries · 19

charouhias:	these shoes form part of the uniform of the evzones, the former Royal Guard of Greece
rose-beetle:	the rose-chafer, a beetle that eats roses
fiesta:	holiday in honour of a saint's day
banked:	imitated the movement of an aeroplane which tilts to one side when turning
the islanders had a love and respect for the Englishman:	following the Napoleonic wars Corfu, which had been under Venetian rule for centuries, became a British possession until 1864 when it was handed over to Greece along with the rest of the Ionian Islands
Achilles:	after the Greek warrior hero who actually figures in a race with a tortoise in a paradoxical fable by the fifth-century BC Greek philosopher Zeno
mumbling:	chewing with toothless gums
emulate:	do better than others
Search-parties:	groups of people organised to look for a lost person
artificial respiration:	reviving of a lifeless person by blowing air into his lungs by mouth and forcing air out of the lungs by pressure on the rib cage
peroxiding:	colouring hair yellow by using the bleach hydrogen peroxide
Quasimodo:	the ugly hunchback bell-ringer of the Cathedral of Notre Dame in Paris in the French writer Victor Hugo's (1802–85) novel *Notre Dame de Paris*
Sousa:	John Philip Sousa (1854–1932), American composer of popular marches

Chapter 4: A Bushel of Learning

Mrs Durrell is worried about Gerry's education. After a long discussion in which each member of the family offers different advice, Larry's friend George is engaged as Gerry's tutor. George soon realises that Gerry's great passion is natural history, and he cleverly manages to introduce animals into lessons on mathematics, history and geography. Some lessons take place in a small bay, enabling Gerry to study the sea creatures at the same time.

NOTES AND GLOSSARY:

Bushel:	old-fashioned measure for grain or fruit (about 36 litres), also used generally to indicate a large quantity
Merchant Navy:	commercial shipping, as distinct from the Royal Navy
hobbledehoys:	clumsy, awkward young men

Rabelais: François Rabelais (?1494–?1553), French satirical writer, author of *Gargantua* and *Pantagruel*. His cheerfully free references to sexual and bodily matters have earned him a bad reputation
advocating cold baths: in the nineteenth century regular cold baths were seen as strengthening a young man's character and keeping him from loose living
brain-wave: clever idea
eulogistic: full of praise
vulpine: fox-like
ransacked: searched thoroughly
Pears Cyclopaedia: a popular one-volume encyclopaedia
from Wilde to Gibbon: Oscar Wilde (1854–1900), witty Irish poet and dramatist; Edward Gibbon (1737–94), English historian, author of *The Decline and Fall of the Roman Empire* (1776–88)
Le Petit Larousse: French illustrated dictionary
agog: eagerly expectant
saturnine: gloomy
Herculean: very difficult, after the Greek hero Hercules who was given twelve hard tasks as a punishment after having killed his children in a fit of madness
gird our loins: prepare for action
flick: quick movement of the hand
foil: fencing sword with a blunt tip
trade winds: winds which blow perpetually towards the equator and are turned westward by the eastward rotation of the earth
tidal wave: an exceptionally high ocean wave, caused, for instance, by an earthquake
galleons: large sailing-ships
jaundiced crews: the little boy colours the faces of the Chinese crews bright yellow as if they were suffering from jaundice, a disease which affects the complexion, turning it yellow
conversant with: well acquainted with
Carter Paterson: large firm specialising in removal of goods or household effects by road
tiger-striping: sunlight entering the room through the horizontal slats of the blinds made a striped pattern
goldfinches: colourful singing-birds of the finch family
hermit crabs: crabs which live in the empty shell of molluscs, soft snail-like creatures
carunculated: covered with small fleshy lumps

'**the French and British Fleets**': this is George's original description of the Battle of Trafalgar (21 October 1805), the decisive sea battle of the Napoleonic wars, won by the British

'**Kiss me, Hardy**': the dying words of Lord Nelson (1758–1805), commander of the British Fleet at Trafalgar. He was fatally wounded during the battle and died in the arms of his old friend Sir Thomas Hardy, Captain of the flag-ship *Victory*

Chapter 5: A Treasure of Spiders

One afternoon Gerry goes off with Roger to the beach. Hungry after his swim he decides to visit the old shepherd Yani, hoping to be offered hospitality there. His hopes are not disappointed, and as they sit eating and talking, Yani tells him about scorpions whose poisonous sting can kill a man. From Yani's cottage Gerry walks to an olive grove where he discovers strange little circular trapdoors in the mossy ground. Excited by his find he rushes off to ask George for an explanation. At George's villa he meets Dr Theodore Stephanides who is an enthusiastic naturalist. Theodore identifies the mysterious trapdoors as the burrows of the trapdoor spider. Two days later Gerry receives a parcel from Theodore containing a pocket microscope, and an invitation to tea.

NOTES AND GLOSSARY:
like a water-picture: like a reflection on water
blennies: shiny fish with spiny fins
virago: mannish, bad-tempered woman
a cast in one eye: a squint
little corn-top: a nickname referring to Gerry's fair hair
deal chair: chair made of cheap soft wood
argued long practice: showed long practice
Saint Spiridion: the name of the patron saint of the island is frequently used by local people as an exclamation of surprise
'**the little ones of God**': small creatures such as insects
'**do damage with his backside**': the scorpion's sting is in his tail
scimitar: Oriental curved sword
mite: tiny spider
bevelled: smoothed off at an angle
Doctor Theodore Stephanides: an army doctor, Dr Stephanides became one of the closest friends of the Durrells, and gave much encouragement to Gerry in his pursuit of zoology. He appears also in Lawrence Durrell's book on Corfu, *Prospero's Cell*, and in Gerald Durrell's *Birds, Beasts and Relatives* and *The Garden of the Gods*

homburg:	a man's soft felt hat with a narrow brim and a dented crown
***daphnia magna*:**	the water-flea
collecting bag:	a naturalist's bag for collecting specimens
***cteniza*:**	the trapdoor-spider (the Latin name of the species is *Ctenizidae*)
Johnny:	(*slang*) fellow, chap
magnification:	power to increase the apparent size of a thing by the use of a lens
***field* work:**	scientific work in the open air, as opposed to the laboratory

Chapter 6: The Sweet Spring

Throughout the winter Gerry visits Theodore regularly, and they examine the various specimens in Theodore's study, discussing what they have observed and looking forward to the spring when they will be able to pursue their nature studies in the open. Spring comes at last, and all the family are affected. Larry takes to drinking wine while singing love songs. Mother gardens and experiments in the kitchen with fresh vegetables. Margo becomes even more interested in fashion and finds a boyfriend, a Turk whom all the family dislike intensely for his conceited self-confidence. Fortunately after a disastrous visit to the local cinema Margo loses all interest in her admirer. For Leslie the arrival of the spring means splendid opportunities for shooting doves.

NOTES AND GLOSSARY:

Sherlock Holmes:	the famous hero of detective stories by Sir Arthur Conan Doyle (1859–1930)
Darwin:	Charles Darwin (1809–82), English scientist, author of *Origin of Species by Means of Natural Selection* (showing that a species of plant or animal develops so as to survive in its environment) and *The Descent of Man* (tracing man's origin back to the apes)
Le Fanu:	Sheridan Le Fanu (1814–73), Irish writer of novels and short stories with a thrilling, often supernatural element
Fabre:	Jean Henri Fabre (1823–1915), French entomologist, nicknamed 'the Insects' Homer'
***ceratophyllus fasciatus*:**	the Latin name for the rat flea, a flea which attacks rats
spinnerets:	web-spinning organs of spiders
***epeira fasciata*:**	the garden spider
tack:	move in a zigzag fashion

cyclops:	tiny freshwater creature with oar-like swimming feet. Its name derives from the one-eyed giants Cyclopes of Greek mythology, because it too has one eye only
cyclops viridis:	the green cyclops
egg-sacs:	pocket-like structures in a female insect's body for storing eggs before they are hatched
Hephaestus:	Greek god of fire
shoulder:	push hard with one's shoulder
tadpoles:	embryo frogs with tails which do indeed resemble drops of water
Salonika:	region round the Greek port of the same name on the Aegean Sea
vampires:	legendary dead men who rise from their graves to suck the blood of sleeping people
Bosnia:	region in central Yugoslavia
vein:	layer of valuable metal running through a rock
vetch:	one of a group of plants of the pea family
cortège:	funeral procession
dyspepsia:	indigestion, stomach ache
bicarbonate of soda:	sodium bicarbonate, taken in water to relieve indigestion
ungulate:	hoofed animal
fatty degeneration of the heart:	disease caused by excessive deposits of fat in the cells of the tissue of the heart
limpet:	snail-like creature which clings to rocks
St Bernard:	large breed of dog
in season:	during the mating period
largesse:	distribution of gifts
chaperones:	older women accompanying unmarried young girls on social occasions
yashmaks:	veils for covering women's faces in public in Moslem countries
double-barrelled:	having two barrels side by side, to be fired quickly one after the other
chairete, kyrioi:	be happy, gentlemen

Conversation

Larry has written to all his friends inviting them to stay. It does not occur to him that the villa is too small to accommodate a number of visitors as well as the family. When this is pointed out to him, he declares that the solution to this problem is to move to a larger house before his friends arrive. The brief chapter ends with Mrs Durrell declaring firmly that another move is out of the question.

24 · Summaries

NOTES AND GLOSSARY:
highbrow: intellectual
phobia: irrational fear
in batches: a few at a time

PART TWO

Motto to Part Two

A quotation from the Bible, Hebrews 13: 2, in which St Paul urges his correspondents to be hospitable to strangers, remembering that sometimes men have entertained strangers who then revealed themselves to be God's angels (as in the Apocryphal Book of Tobit, in which Tobit and his son Tobias welcome the angel Raphael sent to them by God).

Chapter 7: The Daffodil-Yellow Villa

In spite of Mrs Durrell's declared intention to stay where they are, the family move to a larger villa. It is a melancholy, decaying house with a resident gardener whose wife, Lugaretzia, helps out in the house. Lugaretzia is an enthusiastic hypochondriac who drives the whole family mad with her detailed descriptions of her various ailments.

Mrs Durrell goes into town with Gerry and Margo, and they are caught up in a large crowd going to the church to kiss the feet of the mummified Saint Spiridion, the patron saint of the island. Gerry and his mother only pretend to join in this act of worship, but Margo kisses the saint's feet with enthusiasm, and catches influenza.

Gerry explores the garden of the new house, and watches the nesting swallows under the eaves. He finds a strange beetle, identified by Theodore as the oil-beetle.

NOTES AND GLOSSARY:
The new villa was enormous: the comic effect of the simple opening sentence relies on the ending of the preceding chapter, which closes with Mrs Durrell's firm declaration that the family will remain in the pink villa
Venetian: Corfu was under Venetian rule almost continuously from 1386 until 1797 when it was taken over by the French. At the close of the Napoleonic wars Corfu became a British Protectorate. In 1864 Britain handed Corfu over to Greece
scabby: covered with scabs, dried crusts which form over sores
larger intestine: part of the digestive system

ghoul: horrible ghost which feeds on people
fiesta: holiday honouring a saint's day
Saint Spiridion: the procession of the saint's body takes place four times a year: on Palm Sunday before the Greek Orthodox Easter and on the following Saturday, on 11 August and on the first Sunday in November
the consumptive: those suffering from tuberculosis, formerly a deadly disease of the lungs
chrysalis: pupa, the case enclosing an insect in the intermediate stage of development between the larva (the caterpillar, for instance) and the fully developed insect (for example, the butterfly)
threw caution to the winds: became reckless
beef-tea: strong extract of beef, given to invalids
rose-beetles: see notes on Chapter 3
carpenter-bees: see notes on Chapter 2
trapdoor spiders: see description of these insects in Chapter 5
tree-frogs: these are a kind of frog which lives in trees, really of the toad family
goldfinches, greenfinches: varieties of the finch, a singing bird
redstarts: birds with bright chestnut-coloured tails
orioles: golden-yellow birds with black wings
hoopoe: see notes on Chapter 3
wear himself to a shadow: grow very thin
dragon-flies: large long-bodied, brightly coloured insects
ant-lions: insects whose larvae trap ants in specially built holes in the sand
rumba: lively South American dance
bulbous: lumpy
coleoptera: beetles
'backing a horse . . . against you': betting money on a horse which has no chance of winning the race
Smyrna: port on the western coast of Turkey
charger: war-horse
eau-de-Cologne: scented toilet water originally from Cologne in West Germany

---

Chapter 8: The Tortoise Hills

Gerry watches the spring mating of the tortoises on the hills behind the villa. There is a constant stream of visitors at the villa, as Larry's friends arrive and depart. There is the girl-chasing, wine-drinking Armenian poet, Zatopec; three English painters—Jonquil, Durant and Michael—none of whom does any painting while staying at the villa; and the bald Countess de

26 · Summaries

Torro who lost all her hair during an illness. Mealtimes are full of talk and laughter.

NOTES AND GLOSSARY:
emperor moths: large species of moths
mantids: insects which hold their forelegs as if they were praying
goldcrests: very small birds with crests of golden feathers
forage caps: soldiers' caps for ordinary occasions
swallow-tail butterfly: yellow and black butterfly with pointed wing tips
fancy footwork: a boxer's rapid movements round his opponent
broadside: fire from all the guns on one side of a warship
cave-man tactics: the primitive man's rough treatment of a woman
heavy-handed: clumsy, stupid
Madame Cyclops: after the race of one-eyed giants of Greek mythology
sirocco: hot dry wind from North Africa
forty winks: brief sleep
bleeding: euphemism for 'bloody'
asthma: disease of the breathing apparatus, causing difficulties in breathing. It is often caused by an allergy, an abnormal reaction to some ordinary substance
erysipelas: skin disease causing deep redness of the face
of a much more unlady-like character: syphilis, a venereal disease
panama: flat-brimmed straw hat
tenner: (*slang*) ten-pound note
Lawrence: D.H. Lawrence (1885–1930), English novelist. His novel *Lady Chatterley's Lover* was banned in England for many years. Margo is confusing him with T.E. Lawrence (1888–1935), soldier and writer, an enthusiastic supporter of the Arab nations. His work is called *The Seven Pillars of Wisdom*
shibboleths: catchwords, favourite phrases of a particular group
the Battle of Thermopylae: the heroic defence in 480BC of the pass of Thermopylae by a small Spartan army under Leonidas against the Persians led by Xerxes. Through treachery the Persians were able to attack from the rear, and all the Greeks were killed
geckos: species of lizards with adhesive pads on their feet so that they can for instance walk on ceilings

Chapter 9: The World in a Wall

Gerry likes to watch the various creatures which live in the old garden wall, especially the scorpions. One day he discovers there a mother scorpion with a large number of tiny baby scorpions clinging to her back. He places the creature carefully in a matchbox and takes her home. Over lunch he puts the box on the mantelpiece, and his brother Larry picks it up to light his cigarette at table. The enraged scorpion rushes out on to his hand, and pandemonium breaks out. The consequences of this incident are quite serious for Gerry. His mother decides that he is running wild and sends him for French lessons to the Belgian consul, another of Durrell's entertaining eccentrics. Bored with his French lessons, Gerry enjoys all the more his nature walks with Theodore.

NOTES AND GLOSSARY:

crane-flies:	these are a long-legged variety of fly
tessellated:	marked out in small squares
glow-worm:	insect whose wingless female gives out a faint light
hunting-pink:	red riding-coats of the English foxhunters
lacewing-flies:	see notes on Chapter 2
quashed:	annulled, put an end to
cut-away coat:	coat with the skirts cut away in front in a curve, worn on formal occasions
spats:	coverings for shoes which extend over the instep and a little way up the ankle
malacca cane:	brown walking-stick made from the long thin trunk of the rattan palm-tree
as all Englishmen were lords:	see notes on Chapter 3
antimacassars:	ornamental covering for chair-backs, to protect them from hair-oil
Le Petit Larousse:	see notes on Chapter 4
zis:	this; the consul speaks English with a strong French accent
blood feud:	deadly hostility between two families, usually begun as revenge for murder
fusillade:	continuous gunfire
seaplane:	aircraft capable of landing on water, with floats instead of landing-wheels
en route:	(*French*) on the way
grist to our mills:	useful to us
cyclops:	see notes on Chapter 6
caddis larva:	larva of the caddis fly

Chapter 10: The Pageant of Fireflies

Summer comes to the island. Gerry has a new tutor, Peter, an Oxford student who at first tries to follow proper educational methods until the lazy atmosphere of the island, as well as his growing interest in Margo, has its effect on him. Gerry carries on with his nature studies, at night as well. One night he catches a baby Scops owl and brings him home. The owlet is christened Ulysses, and becomes part of the household.

During the hot weather the family bathe in the sea at night, and a special bathing party is organised in honour of Mother's new bathing-costume. The phosphorescent sea, a playful school of porpoises and swarms of fireflies all combine to make the occasion truly memorable.

NOTES AND GLOSSARY:

zithered: played tunes on a zither, a string musical instrument played by the hand
pitted: marked with small holes
crane-flies: see notes on Chapter 9
trying: tiresome, irritating
***Boy's Own Paper*:** popular boys' magazine published between 1879 and 1967
frog-spawn: frogs' eggs
taxidermy: art of preparing and stuffing dead animals to make them appear life-like
cured: preserved by drying
night-jars: goatsuckers, nocturnal birds of the swift family
Scops owl: a species of owl
nonplussed: perplexed, uncertain what to do
Maltese crosses: crosses with the four limbs widening towards the ends which terminate in two points. The Maltese cross was originally the badge of the Knights of Malta, a religious order which provided lodgings for pilgrims to Jerusalem
pelmet: curtain rod with a frill
regurgitate: bring up food from the stomach by the mouth
gambolled: played boisterously
porpoise: fish-like sea animal of the dolphin family
trod water: made walking movements on the spot to keep upright in the water
phosphorescence: quality of shining in the dark
firefly: insect which gives out a light at night
waterlogged: too heavy through being full of water
tiller: handle of the steering mechanism of a boat
Albert Memorial: ornamental monument erected by Queen Victoria in Kensington Gardens in London in memory of her husband, Prince Albert (1819-61)
Perseus's rescue of Andromeda: in Greek mythology Perseus rescued Andromeda, who had been chained to a rock as a sacrifice to a sea monster

Chapter 11: The Enchanted Archipelago

Gerry discovers a large group of small islands particularly rich in sea fauna. As his family refuses to take him there as often as he would like to go, Gerry decides to use his approaching birthday as an opportunity to acquire all the equipment he needs, and especially a boat. He persuades his brother Leslie to build him a small boat which is ceremonially christened the *Bootle-Bumtrinket* on the morning of Gerry's birthday. In the evening a large and enjoyable party is held in his honour. Among his presents are two puppies, christened in spite of Mother's protests Widdle and Puke (because of their lamentable lack of toilet training), who become very much part of the family.

The following morning Gerry, accompanied by Roger and the two puppies, sails his boat successfully for the first time, and returns laden with specimens.

NOTES AND GLOSSARY:
outboard engine: engine fitted to the outside of a boat
archipelago: group of islands
formalin: formic aldehyde, a liquid used for preserving specimens of animals
muzzle-loader: gun loaded through the muzzle, at the end of the gun
steed: horse for riding
dungbeetle: beetle which lays its eggs in dung
was a stickler for procedure: insisted on the correct procedure
Jolly Roger: pirates' flag with a skull and crossbones
Bootle: an endearing combination of 'beetle' and 'boat', in fact the name of a town in Lancashire in the north of England
Bumtrinket: a vaguely rude nonsense name: 'bum' is the colloquial word for the bottom
slipway: sloping pier in a shipyard
turned turtle: turned upside down
Clydeside: then the main Scottish shipbuilding area west of Glasgow
Manx cat: a tail-less breed of cat from the Isle of Man
Widdle and Puke: to widdle means to urinate; to puke means to vomit
Kalamatiano: a Greek folk dance
limericks: humorous five-line poems, often indecent, which usually contain the name of a place
land-lubberish: unused to sea and boats
serpulas: kind of bristly worms with an attached tube
blennies: see notes on Chapter 5

sea urchins:	sea creatures which live inside a round or heart-shaped prickly shell
anemones:	sea anemones, sea creatures which resemble flowers
Medusa:	in Greek mythology one of the monstrous Gorgons, a beautiful woman with snakes instead of hair. Anyone who looked at her was turned to stone. She was beheaded by Perseus who fought her while using a mirror so as not to have to look at her
spider-crabs:	crabs with long thin legs
hermit crab:	see notes on Chapter 4

Chapter 12: The Woodcock Winter

At the end of the summer Peter has to leave, as Mrs Durrell does not approve of his attachment to Margo. Margo locks herself in the attic to mourn dramatically over the loss of her admirer, while consuming large meals brought to her on trays. She returns to normal when Leslie's burglar trap discharges three guns in the middle of the night.

Winter approaches, and Leslie is in his element shooting game and wild birds. He challenges Larry to shoot down two snipe with a double-barrelled gun. Larry fails to perform this feat and falls into the marsh. Soaked to the skin he is brought home and put to bed. While he is trying to ward off a cold with the help of brandy and a good fire in his bedroom, a fire starts in the room. The entire family rush in trying to extinguish the fire, but Larry himself stays in bed and directs the operation.

NOTES AND GLOSSARY:
Camille:	the tragic heroine of Alexandre Dumas the Younger's (1824–95) novel *La Dame aux camélias*. *Camille* was the title of the first English translation of the novel by Sir Edmund Gosse
Tennyson:	Alfred Lord Tennyson (1809–92), the great Victorian poet
closeted:	shut up away from people
twelve-gun salutes:	the ceremonial firing of twelve cannon to mark an important occasion
'Timber':	the traditional warning cry of woodmen when a tree they have been working on is about to fall
one mercy:	one good thing to result from it
sirocco:	see notes on Chapter 8
foundered with all hands:	filled with water and sank with all her crew
skull-cap:	close-fitting cap without brim
whirligiging:	spinning round and round
lake of Butrinto:	in Albania, near the Greek border

snipe:	marshland game bird with a long straight beak
woodcock:	game bird related to snipe
beaters:	men employed by hunters to scare birds or game out of their hiding-places
broke cover:	ran out of its hiding-place out into the open
kicked:	(*of a gun*) jumped violently against the hunter's shoulder when fired
overdraft:	excess of money spent over the amount of money in one's bank account
parlance:	way of speaking
mercurial:	ready-witted
'kill two birds with one stone':	a proverb meaning 'achieve two purposes by one action'
Robin Hood:	legendary English hero, the leader of a band of outlaws who lived in Sherwood Forest in Nottinghamshire, robbing the rich and helping the poor
irrigation ditches:	narrow canals dug to drain excess water from marshland
spreadeagled:	lying on his back with arms and legs outstretched
'sink like . . . Shelley':	the Romantic poet Percy Bysshe Shelley (1792–1822) was drowned off the Italian coast at Lerici
coup de grâce:	(*French*) killing blow administered to a severely wounded creature in great pain
'full fathoms five':	a quotation from Shakespeare's *The Tempest*, I.ii. 394: 'Full fathom five thy father lies'. Even in his misery Larry, like a true writer, speaks in literary allusions
Epsom salts:	magnesium sulphate, used as a purgative
tiddled:	(*colloquial*) drunk
'keep your head . . . losing theirs':	a quotation from Rudyard Kipling's (1865–1936) poem 'If'

Conversation

The family sit on the veranda reading their mail. Margo is studying a fashion magazine, Leslie a gunsmith's catalogue. Larry is reading letters from his artistic friends while Mother reads letters from family relatives. She is suddenly alarmed to discover that Great-aunt Hermione, a very disagreeable old lady, is proposing to come on a visit, believing that there must be room for her in their large villa. Larry finds the solution in this crisis: they must move at once to a smaller house.

NOTES AND GLOSSARY:
'Lead, Kindly Light': a church hymn by Cardinal Newman (1801–90)

32 · Summaries

put away: sent to an asylum for the insane
zombies: the walking dead in West Indian voodoo superstition
'a change is as good as a feast': Margo is mixing up two sayings: 'A change is as good as a rest' and 'Enough is as good as a feast'

PART THREE

Motto to Part Three

A quotation from Nicholas Udall's (1504–56) comedy *Ralph Roister Doister*, the earliest known English comedy.

Chapter 13: The Snow-White Villa

The new villa again has a most interesting garden for Gerry to explore. There are mantids all over the hill on which the villa stands, and in the cracks of its walls there are geckos. As both species live on insects, there is constant war between them. One night Gerry witnesses a long battle between his favourite gecko, Geronimo, and an exceptionally large mantid, Cicely. Geronimo wins in the end and eats up his defeated enemy. Near the villa Gerry discovers two unusually large toads whom he brings home. To his surprise, no-one shares his enthusiasm for his new pets, except Theodore.

NOTES AND GLOSSARY:
pelmet: see notes on Chapter 10
rutted: having deep marks left in the mud by the wheels of vehicles
exquisite: a delicate, elegant person
mantids: see notes on Chapter 8
geckos: see notes on Chapter 8
Geronimo: (?1829–1909) brave leader of the American Apache Indians against the authorities of the United States
viscera: internal organs of the body
proboscis: elongated mouth-part of an insect
daddy-longlegs: crane-fly, see notes on Chapter 9
lacewing-flies: see notes on Chapter 2
walrus moustache: moustache with long drooping ends
drop his tail: lizards are able to discard their tail without suffering an injury
thorax: part of an insect's body that bears the legs and wings
greensward: piece of ground covered with grass
carunculated: see notes on Chapter 4

'to swallow *swords*': a sword-swallower may be seen in a circus; perhaps the idea suggested itself to Theodore while he was comparing the toad to another circus performer, the conjurer
'toad *in a hole*': one of Theodore's dreadful puns: 'toad in the hole' is the name given to a dish of sausages cooked in a batter made of milk, eggs and flour

Chapter 14: The Talking Flowers

Gerry has a new tutor, Mr Kralefsky, a tiny eccentric man passionately devoted to his vast collection of caged birds. Gerry enjoys his visits to Mr Kralefsky's flat very much, though he acquires very little knowledge of conventional school subjects. He meets Mr Kralefsky's mother, a strange old lady with beautiful long hair who tells him that flowers talk to each other.

NOTES AND GLOSSARY:
charlatans: impostors, people who pretend to have knowledge which they do not possess
Hoopoe: see notes on Chapter 3
redstart: see notes on Chapter 7
ornithologist: one specialising in the study of birds
bravado: show of courage
tattoo: series of loud knocks
donning: putting on, dressing onself in
'That's the ticket!': that's exactly what is needed
licheny: like lichen, a moss-like growth on trees and rocks
aviculturist: one who keeps birds
deal: cheap soft wood
goldfinches: see notes on Chapter 4
greenfinches: green song-birds of the finch family
linnets: small brown song-birds
bullfinches: birds with a rose-red breast and a blunt beak
clutch: set of eggs laid at the same time
winged time: time passing quickly as if on wings
groundsel: weed used for bird food
stickler: see notes on Chapter 11
Les Petits Oiseaux de l'Europe: (*French*) a book about ornithology called Small Birds of Europe
Alice in the Looking-glass: In Lewis Carroll's *Alice Through the Looking-Glass* Alice wants to see the garden from the top of a hill, but finds that all the paths take her back to the Looking-glass house

34 · Summaries

limbo:	region on the edge of hell, a place of neglect and forgottenness
'needs must where the devil drives':	we have no choice
loquats:	fruit of a Far Eastern tree of the rose family
Narcissus:	in Greek mythology a beautiful young man who fell in love with his own reflection in a fountain, jumped in and was drowned
Touched:	not quite sound, slightly mad
inaudible to an elderly person:	deafness in old age usually begins with inability to hear the high frequencies of sound
pick-me-up:	tonic, refreshing drink
class distinction:	separation into different social classes
lying in state:	lying in an open coffin in a place of honour before burial

---

Chapter 15: The Cyclamen Woods

While roaming in the cyclamen woods near the villa, Gerry discovers a magpies' nest, and removes two of the babies. The Magenpies, as Spiro calls them, settle down happily in the villa and grow into splendid large birds. They are naturally very inquisitive, and after they have ransacked Larry's room Gerry decides to build a large cage for them. He invites Mr Kralefsky to advise him on the construction of this cage, and during the visit persuades his tutor to teach him wrestling, at which Mr Kralefsky claims to be a master. During the lesson Gerry throws Mr Kralefsky down and breaks two of his ribs.

NOTES AND GLOSSARY:

cyclamen:	plant with beautiful pink butterfly-shaped flowers
conical:	having a wide round base and tapering to a point
Maltese cross:	see notes on Chapter 10
pimpernel:	small red field flower
Arsène Lupin:	hero of Maurice Leblanc's (1864–1925) detective stories who is a criminal as well as a detective
ace of the air:	distinguished airman
understatement:	statement which is too moderate to be fully truthful
Attila the Hun:	(c.403–453) leader of armies of Huns, Vandals and Goths which overran and devastated Eastern and Central Europe and advanced west as far as Orléans in eastern France where they were defeated
a constitutional:	a walk for one's health
Murmansk:	port in northern Russia, on the Barents Sea
mosquito boot:	soft leather boot reaching below the knee, worn for protection against mosquito bites

Neanderthal Man: ape-like prehistoric man, named after Neanderthal, a valley in West Germany where a skeleton of this species was found in 1856
cad: vulgar, ungentlemanly fellow
Anopheles mosquitoes: these are a germ-carrying kind of mosquito

Chapter 16: The Lake of Lilies

Mrs Durrell acquires a puppy, a Dandy Dinmont bitch called Dodo. The dog becomes so attached to her owner that Mrs Durrell is made virtually a prisoner, unable to leave the house, especially after Dodo has had a puppy. Both Dodo and her puppy have to be taken on the annual outing to Lake Antiniotissa when the lilies are in flower there. The family, accompanied by Spiro and Theodore, spend a whole lovely day there, returning home by moonlight.

NOTES AND GLOSSARY:
quarters: lodgings, place where one lives
coasted: drove the dar downhill without starting the engine
decline: state of continuously worsening ill-health
city slickers: clever, dishonest town dwellers
Dandy Dinmont: a breed of terrier, named after Dandie Dinmont, a Scottish farmer in Sir Walter Scott's (1771–1832) novel *Guy Mannering*, who owned two dogs of this breed
Frankenstein: artificial man. In Mary Shelley's (1797–1851) novel of the same name Frankenstein is a young scientist who creates a monster out of corpses from churchyards, but the name is now commonly used to describe a monster such as Frankenstein had made
'before you go throwing stones . . . in *your* eye': again Margo has confused two proverbs: 'People who live in glass houses should not throw stones' (people who have faults of their own should not criticise others) and the biblical 'Why beholdest thou the mote that is in thy brother's eye, but considerest not the beam that is in thine own eye?' (Matthew 7: 3) (why do you notice small faults in others while ignoring your own greater faults?)
'it's an ill-wind . . . moss': the two proverbs which Leslie has deliberately confused to make fun of Margo are: 'It's an ill wind that blows nobody any good' (someone benefits by every misfortune) and 'A rolling stone gathers no moss' (a person who never settles down will never be rich)

36 · Summaries

limpet:	see notes on Chapter 6
came into season:	became sexually excited
met a fate worse than death:	was seduced
the big top:	the circus tent
clarse:	class; Larry is putting on a London Cockney accent
pot-holes:	deep holes in the ground
harpoon:	spear on a rope for killing fish
Battersea Dogs' Home:	home for stray dogs in south-west London
old wives' tale:	unconvincing superstitious belief
brain-wave:	see notes on Chapter 4
wash:	rough water left behind by a moving boat
canebrake:	mass of reeds growing close together
Strauss:	Johann Strauss the Younger (1825–99), Austrian composer of waltzes and light operettas
Tosca:	opera by Giacomo Puccini (1858–1924)

Chapter 17: The Chessboard Fields

Gerry likes to go hunting for specimens in the network of small fields which had been originally salt pans. One day he discovers a pair of water-snakes there. He catches one in his butterfly net, and captures the other one after a long struggle in the canal. His efforts are observed by a pleasant man who turns out to be a convicted murderer of his wife, let out of prison on trust to spend the weekend at home. Gerry likes him very much, and the man gives him a huge, ferocious black seagull, called Alecko. The family are not very pleased with Gerry's bloodthirsty new acquisition, and he has to cage the bird.

NOTES AND GLOSSARY:
salt pans:	basins in which salt is made by evaporation of salt water
the Venetian days:	see notes on Chapter 7
side-tracked:	turned away from one's original purpose
terrapins:	small water tortoises
snipe:	see notes on Chapter 12
oyster-catcher:	black and white sea-bird
dunlin:	red-backed sandpiper, a seashore bird
terns:	birds of the seagull family
silt:	mud and sand deposited by water
crows' feet:	wrinkles at the outer corners of the eyes
albatross:	large, long-winged sea-bird
a Roc:	enormous white bird of Arabian legends. In the *Arabian Nights* a Roc carries Sinbad the Sailor out of the valley of diamonds on his back

the Ancient Mariner:	hero of Samuel Taylor Coleridge's (1772–1834) poem 'The Rime of the Ancient Mariner'. The mariner (sailor) shoots an albatross and so brings down a curse on his ship. All the crew perish except himself, and the curse is only lifted when he blesses all God's creatures in his heart
crossbows:	hand-held weapons for shooting arrows, stones or other missiles; the Ancient Mariner in Coleridge's poem shot the albatross with a crossbow
guano:	bird droppings used as fertiliser
cyclone:	violent revolving wind-storm
bird of ill-omen:	bird which brings bad luck
Hardened old salts:	experienced old sailors
Saint Elmo's fire:	ball of fire sometimes seen round the mast of a ship during a storm. It is caused by a discharge of electricity
tidal wave:	see notes on Chapter 4
hare lip:	split upper lip, a congenital defect causing speech difficulties
club foot:	deformed foot

Chapter 18: An Entertainment with Animals

It is September, and the Durrells decide to give an early Christmas party for all their friends. Gerry has finally succeeded in catching the ancient terrapin he calls Old Plop, and has installed him in a tank with the water-snakes. He decides to make the tank complete for the party by adding some goldfish. The resourceful Spiro produces several of them, and only later does Gerry discover that they had been stolen from the Greek King's residence in Corfu. Unfortunately both the snakes and the terrapin turn out to have a taste for goldfish, and Gerry has to reorganise the tank, putting the water-snakes into the bath for the time being. The Magenpies get drunk on beer and wreck the beautifully arranged dinner table. As the guests arrive Leslie appears dressed only in a towel; he had gone to have a bath only to find the snakes in the bath-tub. While Larry complains of Gerry's various animals, the gull Alecko starts biting the guests' legs under the table, thus offering proof of the truth of Larry's wild tales.

All the animals safely stowed away, lunch progresses happily, with Theodore telling his amusing Corfu stories. After lunch there is a period of rest, followed by a large and delicious tea. Soon it is time for supper. Yet another animal invasion takes place. Dodo, yet again in season, runs in pursued by a large number of village dogs. Peace is restored once the dogs have been driven away, and the party continues by moonlight with more food, wine and happy talk.

NOTES AND GLOSSARY:

milk of human kindness: an often-used phrase, originally coined by the Irish statesman and essayist Edmund Burke (1729-97) in his *Letter to a Noble Lord*: 'These gentle historians . . . dip their pens in nothing but the milk of human kindness'

dog-eared: (*of a book*) with corners of pages turned back from constant use

switched the points: changed the direction; the image is one of trains being moved from one railway line to another

piles: haemorrhoids, painful swelling of the veins in the anus, the back passage in the body

come into season: see notes on Chapter 16

Romeos: admirers, after the hero of Shakespeare's tragedy *Romeo and Juliet*

chutney: spicy relish made with fruit or vegetables and eaten with meat

red-handed: in the act of committing a crime

take our medicine: accept our punishment

'hare . . . *wig*': a pun on 'hair' and 'hare'

Lamb: Charles Lamb (1775-1834), English essayist, author of *Last Essays of Elia* in which the pun is to be found in the story of an Oxford scholar addressing a porter who is carrying a hare

minotaur: in Greek mythology, a bull-headed monster kept by King Minos of Crete in the Labyrinth, a confusing maze of passages, and fed on human flesh. It was killed by Theseus with the help of Minos's daughter Ariadne who fell in love with Theseus

touched: see notes on Chapter 14

perform our ablutions: wash

hamadryads: large poisonous Indian snakes

Saint Francis of Assisi: (1181/2-1226), founder of the Franciscan order of monks, a gentle saint known for his love of animals

rectum: last section of the large intestine, which terminates in the anus

'he's got beasts in his belfry': a joking variant of the phrase 'He's got bats in his belfry', he is mad

'All the nice gulls . . . sailor': another of Theodore's puns, this time based on the similarity of the sound of the word 'gull' and that of 'girl'

'gull and wormwood': a pun on 'gall and wormwood', something extremely bitter (from the biblical 'wormwood and gall', Lamentations 3: 19)

'such depraved birds':	Larry is making a joke about the double meaning of the verb 'to molest'. It can mean 'to pester, annoy' generally, but it can also mean specifically 'to pester with unwanted sexual advances'
gullible:	easily deceived (from the verb 'to gull', to deceive)

The Return

Kralefsky tells Mrs Durrell that he has taught Gerry all he can, and that Gerry should complete his education in England or in Switzerland. In spite of vehement protests from all the children Mrs Durrell decides that it is time to return to England to discuss their finances with the bank, and to decide on Gerry's education.

So all their possessions are packed, the birds put in cages and the dogs on leads, and after passing through the customs with Spiro's help the family say goodbye to Theodore, Kralefsky and the weeping Spiro, and board the ship that takes them to Brindisi. There they take a train which will carry them to Switzerland and on to England. After they have passed through the efficient Swiss border control they find to Mrs Durrell's great indignation that the Swiss official has described them on the pass control card as 'One travelling Circus and Staff', neatly summing up this eccentric and highly entertaining family.

NOTES AND GLOSSARY:
adamant:	determined, not to be persuaded to change
We should soon be back again in Corfu:	this is 1939 and the war is imminent: there will be no going back to Corfu
rag-and-bone merchant:	man who buys and sells scrap material
fluted:	spoke in a high soft voice
tender:	small boat which carries supplies or passengers to a bigger ship
Brindisi:	port on the eastern coast of Italy

Part 3
Commentary

Structure

Students are always being told to distinguish between the plot—the story of the novel—and the structure—the way in which an author chooses to arrange and present the incidents which form the plot. *My Family and Other Animals* is, of course, not a work of fiction (hard as it may be at times to believe this, the Durrell family did exist and did lead its charmed nomadic existence on Corfu for five years) and does not have a plot. Nevertheless the author had to decide on the form in which to present his memories of the island.

Originally he seems to have had in mind a natural history of the island, but once he introduced his family into the book, any simple descriptive form, either moving round the island or following the changes in its fauna and flora throughout the year, became inadequate, and a new form had to be devised which could accommodate both the natural history of the island with its seasonal changes and the Durrell household in which five eccentric individuals pursued with amiable singlemindedness their separate ways.

In his introductory 'Speech for the Defence' Durrell explains that, in order to compress five years of family living into a manageable whole, he was obliged to cut so much that there is very little left of the original chronological order of events in the book. In this description of the way he set about writing his reminiscences of his family's stay on Corfu, however, Durrell does himself less than justice.

In fact, the form which he employs is a subtle one. It combines the simple chronology of events—the Durrells' arrival on Corfu, their moves first to the pink villa, then to the yellow one, and, lastly, to the white villa from which they returned to England—with the rich memories of five years' happiness which attached themselves to various places on the island and to the people who became the Durrells' friends. The chronological sequence breaks as Gerald remembers something that happened later in the same place or to the same animal or person. Thus the description of his first meeting with the pedlar whom he calls the Rose-beetle Man (Chapter 3) leads naturally to a description of the character and adventures of the animals (Achilles the tortoise and Quasimodo the pigeon) which Gerald bought from him. The chapter closes with a vivid picture of the Rose-beetle Man seen for the last time, happily drunk after a fair.

Similarly the introduction of George as Gerry's first tutor (Chapter 4) who develops some highly original teaching methods designed to keep Gerry interested, brings a memory of what had clearly been many happy hours spent sea-bathing between lessons. Again the description in Chapter 11 of the wonderful discoveries made by Gerry in his little boat, the *Bootle-Bumtrinket*, has a quality of richness, of leisurely happiness which tells the reader that the voyage was the first of many, establishing a recurring pattern for every summer that followed.

The rough chronological order, based on the changes of residence to which the Durrells were peculiarly liable, is thus given a continuous rhythm, a sense of people enjoying the same seasonal pleasures year after year: the annual woodcock shoot (Chapter 12); the annual family outing to Lake Antiniotissa to see the flowering lilies (Chapter 16); Gerry's explorations of the cyclamen woods (Chapter 15) and of the old salt pans (Chapter 17).

All these events are shown as part of a continuing family tradition, described within the framework of the year's changing seasons (a form used by many other writers, especially naturalists, from Gilbert White's (1720–93) *Natural History of Selborne* to Gavin Maxwell's (1914–69) *Ring of Bright Water*). The sense of continuity gained by keeping to the ageless pattern of the seasons is very strong, and it comes as a shock to realise that the period covered in Durrell's book only extends to five years, though it is important to remember that a child's time sense is quite different from an adult's, and that to a ten-year-old boy five years must have seemed a lifetime.

An advantage of a strong natural framework such as the seasons of the year is, of course, the freedom it offers to the author to digress, which Durrell uses to the full. The chapter on the Rose-beetle Man, mentioned above, is an excellent example, but there are many others. The woodcock shoots (Chapter 12) in which Leslie, the middle brother, indulges every winter, lead to an entertaining digression on Larry's attempt to emulate his brother's shooting skill, his fall into the mud and his efforts to ward off a cold with brandy, which in turn lead to the fire in his bedroom. Though the next chapter starts with 'Spring had arrived', there is no abruptness in this; after all, spring does follow winter, and so the transition appears entirely natural.

A characteristic of this form of narrative is a certain static quality. The seasons change, the pets grow from babyhood to full maturity and have to be confined (like the destructive Magenpies) or set free (like the owl Ulysses and the pigeon Quasimodo), and some of them die, like the poor tortoise Achilles, but the people in the story remain the same. Larry gets drunk and writes in his room, Leslie is preoccupied with guns, Margo has acne and is endlessly dieting and falling in and out of love, Mrs Durrell cooks and gardens, and Gerry runs wild, pursuing his nature study in spite of various tutors' attempts to impart other, more conventional forms of knowledge. The family's friends do not change either: Yani the shepherd is always full of country wisdom, the delightful Theodore tells his Corfu stories and makes his horrible puns, the maid Lugaretzia moans about her ailments. There is no marked change in any of them, but remembering the comparative brevity of the period covered we can accept this absence of change quite happily. In fact it again reinforces the timeless quality of this world seen through the eyes of a child, in which the only changes are those dictated by the seasons, and the adults remain always the same.

The absence of plot in a book of this nature paradoxically creates a problem for the author. If there is no plot, there is no yardstick by which to measure the relevance of any one incident to the book as a whole. Durrell himself tells in the 'Speech for the Defence' of having to leave out incidents and characters which he would have liked to include in the book (and for some of which he found a use in his other books on Corfu, *The Garden of the Gods* and *Birds, Beasts and Relatives*).

The difficulty is overcome to some extent by the use of the framework of the year's seasons, combined with the changes of location from one villa to the next. The book is divided into three sections, each named after a villa, and the same number of chapters is allocated to each of these sections, moving from spring to summer, to autumn and to winter, and back to spring again. This plan imposes a discipline on the author, and it defines the need to select in order to maintain the pattern of the chapters.

The methodical neatness of these arrangements is all the more noticeable in a book which moves in a leisurely manner, savouring the changes of place and season. Where in a work of fiction we should find an opening, setting out the background of the action, then a change of speed as events move to the climax, and then a slowing down as the action ends in resolution, here we find a space and time of pure happiness, unchanging between its beginning and its end.

The chapter titles, then, serve as markers along this joyful journey in time, each acting as a reminder of some event or recurring sequence of events and painting in a very few words a picture of happiness. Each change of place (which is of course indirectly a reminder of the passage of time) is signalled by a brief chapter, offering the reasons for the change. The business-like purpose of these brief chapters is indicated by their short titles ('The Migration', 'Conversation', 'The Return'). This device, as well as announcing the coming change, stresses the magic quality of the Durrells' life on the island which is implied in the fairy-tale titles of the chapters proper.

Nothing is allowed to spoil the joy of living on this magic island. In this respect certainly a principle of selection seems to have been applied. There are struggles to the death in nature, as for instance in the battle between the gecko Geronimo and the monstrous mantid Cicely in Chapter 13, or in the description of the mating habits of the mantids in the same chapter. Durrell is too much of the true naturalist to gloss over the cruelties of the struggle for survival. Even Leslie's annual slaughter of the game birds is seen as part of this natural process, but there is no place here for the gratuitous cruelty practised by man on animals (a description of the horrible local custom of burying unwanted puppies alive is to be found in *The Garden of the Gods*).

The structure of the book, then, is dictated by its two main subjects: the natural life of the island with its framework of the seasons, and the Durrells' adventurous existence, shaped by their migrations from villa to villa. The absence of a plot enables the author to maintain the even pace of one happy day following another, and any incidents that might spoil the magic atmosphere are kept out. By following roughly the seasonal round, an impression of continuity is miraculously created, turning five years into a timeless golden age.

The theme of nature

The section on 'Man and nature' in Part 1 of these Notes dealt briefly with our changing attitudes to nature. Here we shall examine in some detail the part nature plays in *My Family and Other Animals*. Although in the 'Speech for the Defence' Durrell jokingly accuses his family of taking over his book and more or less preventing him from writing the natural history of Corfu he had planned, the animals have quite successfully resisted any takeover by humans, and the book remains one that could only have been written by a naturalist, admittedly by one with a sharp eye for human behaviour as well, and a splendid sense of humour.

Nature comes into the book in two ways. First, there are Gerry's pets: his dog Roger is his best friend who accompanies him on all his explorations. While on Corfu Gerry acquires two other dogs, the puppies Widdle and Puke, and his mother is also given a dog, the over-demanding Dandy Dinmont called Dodo. Then there are the animals he buys from the Rose-beetle Man: the tortoise Achilles and the pigeon Quasimodo. Creatures which Gerry finds for himself include the owl Ulysses and the two 'Magenpies', magpies whom he steals from the nest, as he stole Ulysses. The black-backed gull, Alecko, given to him by a convict on parole, concludes the list of animals which actually become part of the Durrell household. Other creatures, named and unnamed, are observed often enough and closely enough to acquire entertaining personalities (such as the gecko Geronimo, the one-eyed tortoise Madame Cyclops, or the mantid Cicely).

All these animals provide material for nature study, of course, but they also become part of the large cast of actors and actresses in Durrell's slapstick comedy. They play alongside the human actors, frequently with them, and are described in the same way. This anthropomorphising manner, attributing to animals human reactions and describing their expressions (if the word can be used of, for instance, an insect like the mantid) in human terms, is quite commonly employed by all kinds of writers, both serious and comic, but it comes as a surprise to find it used so frequently by a naturalist. When the Durrells are being driven to the Swiss pension on their arrival in Corfu, their cab is surrounded by barking local dogs eager to attack Roger whom they see as 'an effeminate black canine who rode in cabs' (Chapter 1). A tortoise is laying eggs 'absent-mindedly' but 'with a rapt look on her face' (Chapter 8). The mantid Cicely lands on Gerry's bedroom wall and looks round 'with an air of grim interest, like an angular spinster in an art gallery' (Chapter 13). The huge toads whom Gerry finds hidden under a tree trunk sit looking at him and 'gulping in the guilty way that toads have' (Chapter 13).

There are two qualities to be noticed about all these descriptive phrases: they are funny because of the incongruity of ascribing to these creatures emotions which we see as peculiarly human, and they are successful as descriptions, evoking a very precise image (the toad breathes heavily, swallowing exactly like a person caught in the act of misbehaving).

It should perhaps be added that, with scrupulous impartiality, Durrell also sees animal features in humans: the tall priest at Saint Spiridion's shrine flaps his black robes like a crow (Chapter 7); the artist Jonquil looks like 'a cockney owl with a fringe' while her fellow-painter Michael resembles 'a well-boiled prawn with a mop of dark, curly hair' and the countess is an 'ancient horse' (Chapter 8). Kralefsky bobs up and down 'like a courting sparrow' (Chapter 14). If these descriptions on the whole lack the vividness of Durrell's descriptions of animals, it may be perhaps that the boy Gerry found people generally less interesting, and as a result his memory of them is less sharp.

There are descriptions of nature of another kind. These are the passages recording the boy's minute observations of his surroundings, which are full of painstaking detail, and are presumably based on his carefully kept nature diary. There is little conscious striving for comic effect in these passages; instead we find a constant awareness of the richness of natural phenomena, of their strangeness. There is a feeling of wonder at these treasures offered to the eye.

The descriptions are almost entirely visual, with a strong awareness of the colour and texture of things. The colours of small spiders' bodies match the flowers in which they live; the glossy ladybirds look like freshly painted toys. All these riches are found in an overgrown flowerbed, on a garden wall, in the shallows of the little bay where Gerry has his outdoor lessons with George. The reader is constantly made aware of a child's eye-view, of seeing things from near the ground where the little boy lay in the grass or sat squatting by a stone.

His sense of wonder is matched by his curiosity, by the desire to find the correct explanation for the strange world round him. In Chapter 5 there is a remarkable description of the trapdoor made by the trapdoor spider. The boy notices faint round marks on the mossy bank he is studying. He decides that they cannot be the footprints of an animal because they are too irregularly scattered for the regular pattern of an animal's footsteps. He takes a piece of grass and eventually succeeds in lifting one of the doors to discover a silk-linked shaft into which the door fits perfectly. His excitement at this discovery is great, as is his satisfaction when Theodore provides the correct explanation of the mystery. The passage sums up the fascination which natural phenomena hold for the true naturalist, suggesting also the way in which a discovery leads to a solution and to another problem: here to the question of how the female trapdoor spider distinguishes the footsteps of a male from those of a possible prey. The little boy's reactions to his discovery—and the fact that he made the discovery at all—offer an insight into his great passion, and help readers to understand and share Gerry's wonder and delight.

There are many other descriptive passages, among them the detailed observation of a lacewing-fly laying her eggs (Chapter 2), of the sea-slugs rolling on the sea-bottom (Chapter 4). Others are pure expressions of visual delight, accurate no doubt in describing what the boy sees, but primarily concerned with conveying the beauty of the scene (for instance, the view of the island on a hot summer afternoon which opens Chapter 4, or in Chapter 10, the glittering image of the phosphorescent porpoises in the sea mirrored by the fireflies in the air above).

The latter descriptive passages, as was noted in the section on 'Structure' above (p.40), often help to shape the narrative by drawing the reader's attention to the seasonal round, but, more effectively and significantly, they are a constant reminder of the physical beauty of the island, of its riches which made it a paradise for the little boy.

There is a special magic about islands, and there are many examples in English literature of the power they exercise over the imagination, from Shakespeare's *The Tempest* to Daniel Defoe's (1660–1731) *Robinson Crusoe*, to Robert Louis Stevenson's (1850–94) *Treasure Island*, and to William Golding's (b.1911) microcosm of evil, the island in *Lord of the Flies*. Every island is a small world, enclosed by the sea that surrounds it, and the limitations of space seem to focus one's attention and sharpen one's perceptions. It is, in fact, the ideal subject for a naturalist to study in detail, and for this reason perhaps, as much as for its magic quality, Corfu was the boy Gerry's paradise.

Style

If the structure of a book is defined as the way an author selects and arranges his material to suit his purpose, style is the manner in which he writes, the way in which he chooses his words and puts them together to enhance the effect he is trying to achieve. It bears therefore the characteristic stamp of an author, it is what distinguishes him from other authors. (There are a few writers, such as Laurence Sterne (1713–68), who employ a structure so unusual that it becomes their hallmark as much as their style. The structure of Sterne's novel *Tristram Shandy* with its digressions, flashbacks, pages left blank deliberately, and pages of typographical patterns, remains to this day an inimitable achievement of an eccentric writer of genius, who was mocked or admired according to the prevalent taste of an age.)

If we ask ourselves what had been Durrell's object in writing *My Family and Other Animals*, the answer will be either that he wanted his readers to share his memories of his childhood years in Corfu, or that he wanted to amuse them. Both answers are correct; Durrell is describing his years on the island as vividly as he can so that his readers will be able to share his memories in their imagination, but he is also writing to make them laugh.

To convey the picture he sees in his mind a writer uses words, especially adjectives and adverbs, which describe as accurately as possible the image in his mind. As well as using such words which describe closely and accurately, he will use direct comparisons (or similes) in which an object is compared to another, thereby drawing attention to the quality they both share. A writer will also make use of the metaphor, a figure of speech very like a compressed comparison, in which instead of saying, for example, that a man is as fierce as a lion in a fight, we say simply 'In a fight he is a lion'.

A writer's use of these two stylistic devices is described as his imagery. Durrell's imagery is discussed in some detail below (p.47), as is also his use of humour, the other important element of his style (p.48), but something should now be said about his style in general.

Gerald Durrell writes in an easy, almost colloquial manner, taking an evident pleasure in his use of words. Admittedly this delight in the English language can lead him astray a little at times when, reluctant to discard a single word, he piles up his adjectives, uses strings of verbs and adverbs with evident enjoyment, savouring the flavour of each word. At the same time there is a purpose in his lavish use of words, especially in his descriptions when he is trying to convey an image in all its richness and subtlety.

Naturally, as there is a large cast of characters in *My Family and Other Animals*, there is a lot of dialogue, and the reader will derive a lot of pleasure from Durrell's skilful reproduction of different people's typical ways of speaking. Apart from the more obvious, though no less entertaining eccentricities of speech, such as Spiro's determined addition of 's' to almost every word of English, or Theodore's hesitant pauses and his puns, there is Margo's gushing girlishness, Leslie's gruff short sentences, Kralefsky's constant use of English idiom ('That's the ticket!', 'By Jove!') which seems, by contrast, to emphasise the little man's peculiar background of 'an intricate tangle of nationalities' (Chapter 14). Mrs Durrell's manner of speaking with its italicised emphases, so characteristic of an English lady, is caught to perfection, as is Larry's swearing, his cavalier dismissal of anything that does not interest him, and his wit. Significantly, no direct speech of Gerry's is recorded anywhere in the book, as if to stress his passive role of observer and recorder.

Direct speech is used to make the reader laugh, to advance the action and indirectly to define the speaker's character. It stands in contrast to the descriptive passages, helping to maintain a balance between the author's twin aims, to describe what he remembers so vividly, and to entertain his readers. Some of the most amusing passages in the book are the conversations.

Durrell is successful in writing dialogue because he is aware of a character's peculiarities which are reflected in his or her manner of speaking, and is able to make use of their comic potential. There is no jarring contrast between the colloquial dialogue and the descriptive sections of the book because Durrell's style is always easy and unaffected. Even his richest descriptive passages are written in good plain English, and are certainly no 'purple patches' of elaborate prose. Perhaps we have his unconventional schooling to thank for this, and Larry's determined policy of exposing his youngest brother to the best in English literature from an early age. Whatever the reason, the book is a joy to read.

Imagery

It is a mistake to assume that to write well, using the resources of the English language to the full, one has to strive after effect, using words and phrases such as will never be found in ordinary speech. An image is successful if it makes the reader see or hear what the writer is seeing or hearing in his imagination, and this can only be achieved if words are chosen because they convey the mind picture accurately, not because they are rare and beautiful in themselves (though of course a beautiful and 'poetic' word may well be the most appropriate one for the writer's purpose).

Durrell's book is packed with images which paint visual and sound pictures. His descriptions are full of similes and metaphors because, while writing for his own and his readers' pleasure, he has the naturalist's urge to describe. He avoids scientific terms and the natural historian's jargon, while making painstakingly sure that his descriptions are accurate and true. The result of this double purpose in his writing is unusual and delightful. He is not constricted by seriousness of purpose, and so can cheerfully describe a hermit crab with an anemone on its shell as being 'like a bonnet with a pink ribbon on it' (Chapter 4). The green tree frogs seem like 'delicious satin sweets' of everyone's childhood, hanging in the trees (Chapter 8). Tortoises emerging from their shells 'unpacked their heads and legs' before setting off 'doggedly and without enthusiasm' (Chapter 3). A scarlet mite struggles through the moss like 'a tubby huntsman' (Chapter 5). The comic effect is as evident here as the accuracy of the observation and the inclination to see—or at least to describe—the world of nature in human terms.

The multitude of metaphors and similes heaped up in joyful profusion in the descriptive passages shows the author's delight in what he sees and hears in his memory. Though visual images predominate, Durrell uses his ears as well, and so the 'newly enamelled' frogs snore rapturously in the ditches, and the echo of the hunters' guns sounds 'like the crack of a great branch in a still forest' (Chapter 6).

However, in the author's eagerness to share his pleasure with his readers there lies a danger; at times we are aware of a repetitiveness, as simile follows simile. The sleeping shepherd Yani's moustache moves like a seaweed in the swell of the sea, his thick yellow finger nails resemble flakes of wax cut from a candle, his face is wrinkled like pine bark, while his wife's is 'as red as a pomegranate seed' (Chapter 5). Again, in the pink villa there are roses with petals like saucers, marigolds 'like broods of shaggy suns', pansies with 'velvety and innocent faces', fuchsia flowers 'like ballerinas' (Chapter 2). The reader's slight irritation soon passes, giving way to a renewed willingness to accept Durrell's invitation to share the sights and sounds he remembers so well.

Humour

Durrell's imagery delights and instructs, by what we instinctively recognise as the aptness of the similes and metaphors, and by the author's evident pleasure in the words he uses. The book's other sources of continuous enjoyment for its readers is the author's sense of humour, which shows itself in several ways.

First, there are the set pieces of slapstick comedy, such as the arrival at the Swiss pension which the Durrells enter pursued by a pack of local dogs (Chapter 1); the cinema visit with Margo's Turkish admirer (Chapter 6); the scorpion family let loose from its matchbox at lunch (Chapter 9); the dog Roger attacking Mrs Durrell's bathing-costume (Chapter 10); or the fire in Larry's bedroom after the snipe shoot (Chapter 12). In all these passages a comic situation is made funnier still by the family's reactions. Either they try desperately and ridiculously to maintain an appearance of normality (Chapters 1, 6) or they react wholeheartedly, each member of this extraordinary family behaving in his or her own characteristic way and so adding to the hilarious confusion, as in the scorpion scene in Chapter 9, or in the panic over the fire in Chapter 12.

Here it should be added that, since every family member usually reacts in the same characteristic manner, the scenes, however entertaining, are to some extent repetitive. It is, however, a fact well known to, say, writers of television comedy series that there is considerable comic potential in a character reacting again and again in the same predictable way. The audience waits for the predictable habitual reaction and laughs with delight when it comes.

Second, Durrell frequently uses the trick of presenting the reader with a twist which by its unexpectedness turns an ordinary situation or saying into an amusing one. Thus, when Mrs Durrell reproaches the children for their selfishness, Larry replies, 'Well, we didn't get as selfish as this without *some* guidance' (Chapter 2). Similarly, in the introductory 'Speech for the Defence' after the author has acknowledged 'the help and enthusiasm' of his family and friends in the making of the book, he adds that he is mentioning this 'so that blame can be laid in the right quarter'. In Chapter 1, and again in Chapter 7, Mrs Durrell's firm refusal to move is followed, deliberately without any explanation, by a family removal; the sequence of firm refusal followed by complete capitulation is a piece of delightful comedy.

Some of the fun in the book comes from Durrell's habit (mentioned above in the section 'The theme of nature', p.43) of ascribing to animals reactions which the reader recognises as purely human, as for instance in the description of the male swallows' contributions to nest-building (Chapter 7) or in the male tortoises' fight for the female and their clumsy mating (Chapter 8). Here the humour lies in the actual description rather than in the situation: the thought of tortoises 'inflamed with passion', gulping and glaring is funny where a matter-of-fact description would not be.

This, of course, is an adult's amusement; the comic scenes in the book, as well as the verbal humour, are the expression of the grown-up Gerald's amusement when he looks back and sees the comic aspect of a situation he had observed as a little boy. In this respect the book presents the reader with a puzzle: to what extent is the author superimposing his adult perceptions, especially in seeing the comic side of a situation? In the hilarious scorpion scene in Chapter 9 young Gerry's natural reaction would be a mixture of alarm at the possible consequences of the incident to himself and of scientific curiosity about the behaviour of the scorpion family. Only later does the adult Durrell add the farcical element with his description of the noisy pandemonium at the lunch table.

This brings us to another aspect of Durrell's humour, his sly asides. In the scorpion scene he remarks that when Roger in his confusion bit Lugaretzia, 'this did not help matters much' (Chapter 9). When the puppies, Widdle and Puke, mess up the dining-room, they leave it 'decorated in a fashion that left us in no doubt that [they] had both eaten and drunk to their hearts' content'. At the launching of Gerry's boat Peter, 'clad in his only decent suit . . . disappeared with scarcely a splash' (Chapter 11).

In all these remarks, delivered with pretended seriousness, the reader is invited to share the author's amusement (again an adult attitude) which adds to the entertainment through the contrast between the outrageous ridiculousness of the situation and the modest, quiet comment, delivered with the tongue firmly in the cheek.

Once more, the humour is basically verbal, since it is the matter-of-fact aside that brings out the comedy of the situation. Durrell's pleasure in using the English language, so evident throughout the book, produces any number of delightful jokes: the male tortoise, unsuccessful in his mating, 'simply folded himself up in his shell and lay there mournfully. The female, meanwhile, ate the dandelion leaf' (Chapter 8); Mother's bathing-costume is an 'airship of frills and tucks' (Chapter 10); the puppy, Dodo, lies in Mother's arms 'like a dimly conscious sausage' (Chapter 16).

The large number of instances in which a simple well-chosen word or phrase changes a plain description into a joke indicates plainly the author's skill with words and his sense of humour which pervades the whole book.

Characters

Gerry

As the 'I' narrator of the book, the little boy Gerry is obviously the most important person in it, but in trying to assess his character we come up against the problem already mentioned in the section on 'Humour' above (p.48). This is a difficulty common to most books of childhood reminiscences: to what extent are the recollections genuine, and how much have they been refashioned by the adult who is now writing them down? Obviously the way a person remembers his past, selecting, even if unconsciously, what he wishes to remember, is a clue to his adult character, revealing his adult interests and attitudes quite as much as those of his childhood self, if not more.

Some writers succeed in standing back and letting the child remember. Charles Dickens (1812–70) rather surprisingly achieves this detachment in his autobiographical novel *David Copperfield* which captures in its early pages the bewilderment of a small child in an incomprehensible adult world. (Thus, characteristically, little David never realises that the 'Brooks of Sheffield' of whom his prospective stepfather, Mr Murdstone, is speaking, is himself. The conversation is reported as the boy heard it, without any comment or explanation.) Such ability, however, is rare, and Gerald Durrell does not possess it, nor, to be fair, is he striving for it. His honest purpose is to entertain, not to build up a complex picture of a small boy in a strange world.

Instead, he gives us a bright, idealised view of the island and of the people living there. It is seen through Gerry's eyes, especially when it comes to the animals and plants of the island. The accuracy of these descriptions is not to be doubted. The boy is a passionate naturalist, with the true scientist's gift for detailed observation, and this aspect of his character is clearly shown. His talent for observation is equally manifest whether he is describing a toad eating a worm (Chapter 13) or the ornate pomp of a Greek funeral (Chapter 1).

His relations with his family can only be guessed at. He loves and largely trusts his mother, the only one in the family to realise the strength of his obsession with the natural world. For his brothers he has a wary respect, based on his awareness of the trouble they could cause him, while Margo he dismisses as no danger to his pursuits. We can only presume that his affection for his siblings is there, as it is never shown; in this respect Durrell shows himself an accurate observer of children's attitudes.

The boy is much younger than his brothers and sister and therefore has the solitary habits of an only child; his dog Roger is his one beloved companion.

He appears to be a likeable, outgoing boy, the first in his family to learn Greek and to form friendships with the neighbours. They nickname him 'little lord', 'little corn-top' (because of his fair hair which is unusual in Greece), and treat him kindly because he is a child and a stranger.

He has great physical courage, shown in his fight with the water-snake in Chapter 17, and in his victory over the fierce black-backed gull Alecko. Like a true naturalist he is not at all fastidious, and finds all creatures interesting and beautiful. The toads which make Spiro sick are lovely to him, and he genuinely cannot understand why other people do not share his admiration for them (Chapter 13).

That he is sensitive to beauty cannot be doubted: the vivid pictures of the island would not have stayed in Durrell's mind if they had not impressed him deeply when he was a child. He has imagination too; the chapter describing how he made the acquaintaince of Kralefsky's mother has the strange dream-like quality of a fairy tale (Chapter 14).

In all it might be said that we see as much of the boy Gerry as the grown-up Gerald allows us to see, and enough to form quite a clear picture of this little boy with an extraordinary passionate interest in nature which has remained with him.

Mother

My Family and Other Animals is dedicated to the author's mother, and his love for her shines through the book. Mrs Durrell is indeed a remarkable woman. She is devoted to her children, and their welfare is foremost in her mind. Typically, when she hears that the house is on fire (Chapter 12) she shouts 'Wake Gerry', and when Leslie's guns go off in the middle of the night she is distraught, thinking that Margo has committed suicide (Chapter 12).

Her manner is always gentle though firm. After their disastrous visit to the cinema with Margo's Turkish suitor, Mrs Durrell remarks mildly: 'I'm afraid you'll just *have* to choose your boyfriends more carefully in the future, Margo' (Chapter 6). When Leslie's guns go off, all she says is, 'You mustn't do things like that, dear . . . it's really stupid' (Chapter 12).

She strives to maintain her dignity in all situations. Like the true English gentlewoman, she resorts to small talk to smooth over a difficult situation, quite unaware of the comic effect of her flow of polite phrases. Her desperate attempts to cover up her sons' rudeness to Margo's Turkish admirer in Chapter 6 are pure comedy ('Lovely having you . . . do have a scone') and offer a very accurate rendering of English table talk, as does her habit of stressing a word now and again in the flow of her soothing murmur of platitudes ('days simply *fly* past').

Her children's outrageous outbursts are met with a gentle reprimand not to be vulgar and a hasty change of subject, but she can be as stubbornly unconventional as they, and quite unaware of her eccentricity, as in her choice of a bathing-costume in Chapter 10, or in her brilliant solution to the problem of Dodo's divided loyalties in Chapter 16.

She alone in the family understands Gerry's obsession with animals which she shares to some extent. (She and Gerry jointly buy up the Rose-beetle Man's entire stock of rose-beetles and set them free 'in a fit of extravagant sentimentality'—Chapter 3.) She is able to receive all the little boy's strange additions to the household with placid words of approval and a real concern for their welfare.

Vaguely benign, she is nevertheless amazingly practical; when the inadequacy of the pension's sanitary arrangements is discovered she at once sets about finding a house with a proper bathroom. She manages her unruly household successfully, copes with a stream of visitors, and, with the help of local girls and the faithful Spiro, organises large parties and cooks all the delicious food herself. Cooking and gardening appear to be her only interests apart from her family, and though her own affections are centred entirely on her children, she inspires a deep regard and instinctive respect in all the people she meets in Corfu.

Margo

The eighteen-year-old Margo is regarded by her youngest brother with amused tolerance. She is preoccupied with her appearance, endlessly trying out new diets to lose weight, and new creams to improve her complexion. Her reading consists of fashion magazines which she studies with great concentration.

Her girlish enthusiasms are mocked by her brothers, and her boyfriends are treated with scorn. She has the teenage girl's talent for self-dramatisation, reacting to every family crisis like the tragic heroine of a melodrama.

When Peter, Gerry's tutor, is sent away because he is becoming too fond of her, she locks herself in her room to mourn — while consuming large meals brought up by Gerry on a tray. This same practical streak reveals itself when she stays too long on an island, indulging romantic thoughts on love, gets sunburnt and has trouble returning home.

She is a non-literary member of this family of writers, mixing up proverbs and confusing one writer with another. There is courage in her determined preoccupation with frivolities in the face of her brothers' mockery, which makes her likeable; one has to admire her persistent efforts to make herself into a romantic figure under such difficult circumstances — a conventional person in a family of eccentrics. Obviously her youngest brother is now aware of his sister's kindly tolerance. He has dedicated his book *The Picnic and Suchlike Pandemonium* to her because she 'has let me lampoon her in print, with great good humour'.

Larry

Perhaps because there is an instinctive affinity between Gerry and his eldest brother (both became successful writers, though in very different fields), or perhaps simply because of Larry's colourful personality, we are given a much clearer picture of this eldest brother. Variously described as 'a small blond firework' ('The Migration'), 'small, portly and immensely dignified' (Chapter 12) — all the Durrells seem to be small — he is a great organiser, but not a doer.

His passion for literature is genuine, and like most people totally dedicated to a subject he cannot imagine anyone not sharing this passion. Thus we find him recommending *The Elizabethan Dramatists* to his mother ('Conversation'), and reproving her for not reading anything except cookery books, gardening books and detective stories.

He delights in being outrageous ('Nothing short of a bayonet would do [Lugaretzia's] stomach any good' — Chapter 7; 'It'll [Mother's bathing-costume] probably suit you very well, if you can grow another three or four legs to go with it' — Chapter 10; 'now we are expected to wade about the house knee deep in guano' — Chapter 17). He prides himself on his unconventionality, recommending that Margo should go and live with Peter as the best way to cure her of her infatuation (Chapter 12), and that his little brother should be brought up on a diet of good literature such as Rabelais (Chapter 4). All this is, of course, just part of his chosen rôle as the bohemian man of letters, as are his wine drinking and singing of melancholy Elizabethan love-songs to mark the coming of spring (Chapter 6).

His pleasure in words and his wit both take the form of cutting, mocking remarks, made distinctive by his imagination. Thus when he is complaining of the thieving Magenpies he describes them as 'flapping round the house with hundred drachma notes in their filthy beaks' (Chapter 15), and when his mother and Margo return at last from the cinema visit with Margo's Turk he pretends to be surprised to see them, remarking that the family had imagined them in Constantinople by now, riding on camels, 'with [their] yashmaks rippling seductively in the breeze' (Chapter 6).

His superior airs, his conviction that he always knows best what to do (as well as the fact that, given that he always puts his own comfort first, he does seem to know the way out of any difficulty) make him a little hard to bear at times, but his resourcefulness, his wit and his evident capacity for enjoyment make up for his shortcomings.

Leslie

Like Margo to some extent, Leslie does not seem to fit into the family, except by virtue of his singleminded passion for guns and hunting. Unlike the rest of the family he is not talkative, except if provoked (usually by Larry) or, if describing a shoot, when he, too, displays a skill with words.

He seems to have inherited his father's technical ability, constructing elaborate gun traps for burglars, and building Gerry's remarkable boat entirely by himself. His view of life is rather like Margo's, conventional and inclined to the melodramatic as when he threatens to shoot Margo's boyfriend Peter (Chapter 12). His swearing, for which he is constantly reprimanded by his mother, is a part of his manly posture, by means of which he is struggling to establish himself as worthy of notice in this extraordinary family. That he is not successful in this is indicated by the relatively small part he plays in the book, the overlooked middle brother.

Spiro Hakiaopulos

One of the most likeable and amusing characters in the book, Spiro is described by the author in some detail. He is short, solidly built, with huge hands and a deceptive scowl on his face. In fact he is the most tenderhearted of men, devoted to Mrs Durrell and deeply shocked by her children's disrespect towards their mother. From their very first meeting, when he saves them from the pressing attentions of the local taxi-drivers, Spiro is the Durrells' guardian angel. He finds a villa with a bathroom for them, supervises the removal of their luggage, and makes sure that nobody cheats them. He is totally honest, ready to challenge authority, and is especially enraged by any display of petty officialdom. When he discovers that the local customs officials have confiscated the cases containing the Durrells' household linen, his indignation and scorn are such that the customs men are subdued into handing over the cases at once.

His fatherly concern is aroused when Margo secretly acquires a Turkish admirer. Like many Greeks he distrusts Turks, and is ready to avenge Margo, should the Turk injure her in any way.

It is hard to imagine how the Durrells could have managed on the island without him. He is a great 'fixer' who knows everyone on the island, and he is generally liked and respected: the Durrells turn to him in any crisis and are never disappointed. He secures the services of the Greek King's ex-butler for the Durrells' party (Chapter 11), catches and cooks fish for their picnic (Chapter 16) and steals goldfish for Gerry from the King's garden (Chapter 18).

As far as the Durrells are concerned one of his most valuable assets is his command of English. Having lived in the United States for a number of years he speaks English quite well in his own highly individual way, adding an 's' at the end of nearly every word. When his weak stomach betrays him at the sight of Gerry's toads, he apologises with a splendid display of final 's's': 'when I sees one of them bastards I haves to throws, and I thought it was betters if I throws out theres than in heres' (Chapter 13).

Though he is proud of being Greek, he has a soft spot for the English, 'best kinds of peoples' (Chapter 1), and goes so far as to declare 'Honest to Gods, ifs I wasn't Greek I'd likes to be English' (Chapter 1).

It is easy to see why the entire family came to depend on him and to see in him a valued friend. His kindness and ability to cope with any awkward situation are unquestionable, and so is his honesty, though his candid way of speaking can be disconcerting at times (as in his scandalised comment on Dr Androuchelli's large family in Chapter 11: 'Gollys! Carrying on like cats and dogses.'). By the end of the book we find ourselves sharing the Durrells' affection for their guide and friend.

Dr Theodore Stephanides

Theodore's friendship for the boy Gerry is of great importance. He understands and shares the boy's passion for natural history, and is able to help him by providing him with books, giving him a microscope, and especially by listening to him, discussing his finds with him, and giving a scientific explanation for any puzzling discovery that Gerry makes. From the very beginning of their friendship he treats Gerry as an adult, shakes hands with him when they are introduced, listens to his excited description of the trapdoor spider's passage, and offers to go and inspect it at once to confirm his own explanation of the strange phenomenon. Characteristically, he gives the spider its Latin name, and so begins to teach Gerry how to study systematically.

We hear a great deal about Theodore in the course of the book, and are given a full description of this remarkable man. He is evidently still a young man, but curiously formal and old-fashioned in his appearance. He has a blond beard, which he rasps with his thumb when he is embarrassed or absorbed in thought, bushy eyebrows, twinkling blue eyes, and a humorous mouth. He is always impeccably dressed in a suit with a waistcoat and a spotless white shirt. His boots are highly polished, and he wears a homburg hat. His manners are formal: he shakes hands on leaving, and thanks his host for his hospitality.

His slow, hesitant speech is due partly to his shyness, but partly also to a striving for dramatic effect, especially when he is about to produce one of his puns (his encounter with Alecko the gull inspires several of them, causing Larry to compare him to an old copy of *Punch*, a magazine which used to be famous for its punning jokes). Obviously he speaks perfect English or he would not be able to make such puns. Lawrence Durrell in his book on Corfu, *Prospero's Cell*, which is dedicated to Theodore among others, describes him at length, and mentions the interesting fact that he speaks Greek with an English accent. As an army doctor he may have, perhaps, trained in England.

As well as punning, Theodore also likes to tell stories about Corfu and its inhabitants, delighting in their absurdities. Though Gerry is his special friend and they meet weekly to study natural history together, Theodore is obviously popular with all the Durrells and soon becomes one of the family.

The author's affection for him is obvious: all Theodore's quirks, such as his passion for watching the weekly landing of the seaplane from Athens (Chapter 9), are described in affectionate detail, conveying clearly the author's liking, admiration and gratitude to this remarkable man.

John Kralefsky

To an adult, Kralefsky and his mother might seem strange, even pathetic figures, but to a little boy all adults are odd anyway, and so he accepts their strangeness in an unsentimental, matter-of-fact way. Gerry notices that his tutor's appearance is unusual, but decides at once that Kralefsky must be a gnome in disguise. The tutor has a large, egg-shaped head which slopes backward to his hunchback, so that he looks as if he were looking upward and constantly shrugging his shoulders. His eyes are very large, sherry-coloured, and give the impression that he is just waking up from a trance. His hands are large for so small a man, with beautifully manicured nails.

Although his surname indicates a Slavonic, possibly Polish ancestry, he is still predominantly English, and as if to stress this he makes constant use of colloquial English phrases ('That's the ticket!', 'By Jove!', 'Needs must when the devil drives'), and tries to organise a cricket match.

He has two great loves in his life, his mother, and his birds (of whom he has a great number, all housed in a specially adapted attic and lovingly tended by himself). He is a lonely man, partly at least because of his strange appearance, but he is not unhappy, having created for himself a rich imaginary world in which he has many adventures, always centring on a Lady in distress whom he rescues through his courage, agility and strength.

Gerry is too young to understand fully that Kralefsky's adventures are simply his way of compensating for his loneliness and poverty (his suits are 'antiquated', the carpets in his flat are 'mangy'), and so he persuades his tutor to give a demonstration of one of his skills, that of wrestling. The demonstration ends badly when Gerry throws Kralefsky as instructed and manages to crack two of his ribs. No permanent damage results, and Kralefsky resumes his dreaming.

It seems that both he and his mother have withdrawn from life, he to dream of splendid adventures and she to lie in bed, admiring her lovely long hair, remembering her former beauty and talking to the flowers with which her loving son fills her room. Their withdrawal from reality seems to make the oddities of both mother and son acceptable, as if they had deliberately chosen to become part of a fairytale world.

Yet Kralefsky follows the rules of everyday life, carefully setting his watch to time Gerry's lessons, teaching the boy history, algebra, geography, all by the dullest and most old-fashioned methods possible, and in the end honestly advising Mrs Durrell that he has taught the boy all he can. His effect on Gerry's education is negligible, but perhaps meeting him and his mother made Gerry aware of the power of imagination.

George

A friend of Larry's, and, like Larry, a would-be writer, George by praising Corfu in his letters is responsible for the Durrells' coming to the island. He becomes Gerry's first tutor. He is an odd-looking man, tall and thin, bearded, with a skull-like face. He has a dry, sarcastic manner which disconcerts his pupil at first, but it seems that he understands the boy's obsession with natural history, and sensibly uses it to make other branches of knowledge more palatable. Thus in geography Gerry draws maps full of pictures of local animals for each region, and in his history lessons animals crop up in the most unexpected places: on landing in America Columbus meets a jaguar, and Lord Nelson bequeathes to Captain Hardy his collection of birds' eggs. No doubt it amuses George to add such items to conventional teaching material, but his method shows considerable sympathy and understanding which make George's lessons a pleasure to his pupil. And George is responsible for introducing Gerry to Theodore who becomes the boy's invaluable guide to the study of nature.

Yani the shepherd

In his rambles through the neighbouring countryside Gerry makes many friends among the Greek peasants, including old Yani who tends his large flock of goats in the hills. He and his wife symbolise the simplicity, generosity and kindness of the Greek people. Yani is amused by the 'little lord', and especially by his interest in 'the little ones of God', the insects, and enjoys instructing the boy in country wisdom and superstition, always speaking to him in a polite, kind manner. From him Gerry learns courtesy and respect for others, qualities which were perhaps largely missing in the Durrells' noisy, entertaining household.

Lugaretzia

Wife of the gardener in the daffodil-yellow villa, Lugaretzia becomes Mrs Durrell's maid and helper. She is a thin, elderly woman, extremely sensitive to criticism, and always ready to burst into tears. She is a hypochondriac, on the lookout for a victim to whom she can describe her latest symptoms in full revolting detail. In this respect it is perhaps unfortunate that one of her jobs is to bring the members of the family their early morning tea, a heaven-sent opportunity for her to treat them all individually to a full description of her ailments. Larry especially objects to this, complaining loudly.

As well as a hypochondriac, Lugaretzia seems to be a hysteric, adding her voice to any family crisis. Her gloomy disposition makes her coquettish response to the attentions of the Armenian poet Zatopec all the funnier. Unlike, say, Spiro or Kralefsky she is literally a figure of fun, and has no function in the book other than to make us laugh.

Part 4
Hints for study

Studying the text

Your first reading of *My Family and Other Animals* should be for enjoyment. Read it right through and enjoy the fun. When you have finished the book, however, think about it a little, and if possible make a few notes. Write down what you liked best, which incidents made you laugh, which characters made the strongest impression on you. There is no need at this stage to express your thoughts in language suitable for the examination room. Just jot down your random ideas.

Read these notes before you embark on your second reading of the book: already you may notice that certain aspects of the book had engaged your attention more fully during the first reading. For instance, you may find that the incidents that made you laugh most all centred on the Durrell family dealing with a crisis in its own inimitable way — a slapstick comedy, in fact. Again, you may find that what you enjoyed most were the detailed descriptions of small creatures going about their business, or perhaps the passages conveying the beauty of the island at different times of the year.

Take your notes quite seriously: they sum up your first impressions, point to what appeals to you most in the book. These are the areas on which you might now wish to concentrate in more detail. After all, in any essay or examination answer you will be giving your own views, backed by a thorough study of the book. If the humour of the book is what you enjoy most, then obviously a question on Durrell's humour will be your best choice, and you should give some thought to that side of the book. Again, if you have enjoyed Durrell's descriptions, you may wish to study his style in more detail. (Remember, however, that in your study you must never concentrate on only one aspect of the book. A thorough knowledge of the text will be expected of you, and skimming through in search of passages relevant to one aspect only is a dangerous practice.)

As well as your personal preferences, you should at this stage consider the book as a whole and try to decide which aspects of it you might be expected to discuss. For instance, in a book like *My Family and Other Animals* the various eccentric characters both inside and outside the Durrell family play a significant part, and you should pay attention to them.

The book is not a novel and has no plot. How does this affect its structure? Look over the contents page and try to remember how the action moves forward in time and in place.

The title of the story is *My Family and Other Animals*; what does this tell you about the book? 'My family' falls under the heading of 'Characters'; what about 'Other Animals'? Durrell's passion for the world of nature is self-evident, but you might consider what forms it takes: animals as pets or animals as subjects of study?

There are many descriptive passages in the book, some dealing with a small area—a garden wall, a grassy bank—others painting landscapes and seascapes, as well as the wide sky above. What means does the author use to make his descriptions come alive for the reader? These are questions of style, of a writer's imagery.

It is a very funny book, but how does the author go about his business of making us laugh? By presenting comic situations, by the witty remarks made by the characters, or by describing people and animals so as to make us see them as funny? A consideration of Durrell's humour is yet another aspect of the book which might be the subject of an examination question.

First, define for yourself the aspects of the book which appeal to you personally. Then think of the book as an examination paper or essay subject and try to decide what form the questions may take. Compare your impressions of the book, jotted down after your first reading, with those aspects of it which you think might come up in examination questions, and decide on which of these you might wish to concentrate in the light of your own personal preferences. You may change your mind completely, or at least modify your plans to some extent, as you proceed with your second reading, but it is useful to have some idea of your strategy at this stage.

It may seem cold-blooded and calculated to view a book purely as examination material, and you may feel that such treatment must destroy your enjoyment of it. Most students think this way, sharing the poet William Wordsworth's (1770–1850) view that 'We murder to dissect' (in his poem 'The Tables Turned'), that is, we destroy a work of art by analysing it. This is not necessarily true: if by thinking about how a book is put together, by trying to define the author's purpose and the means by which he achieves that purpose, we become more fully aware of the parts that come together to form a book, of the author's craftsmanship in putting together these parts, far from being impoverished our pleasure in reading the book should be increased.

We analyse, but we also synthesise; we identify the technique but we still return to reading the book as a whole, our appreciation of it enhanced by our awareness of the skill and thought that has gone into the making of it.

Having thought about the book and your approach to it, you are now ready to move on to your second reading. First, however, you may find it useful to write down a few headings relevant to the aspects of the book which interest you. For instance, if you feel you would like to discuss Durrell's humour, decide what form it takes: comic situations, witty conversation, amusing descriptions, and so on. Take a sheet of paper and divide it into columns headed by the aspects of Durrell's comic writing which you have identified (say, HS for humorous situation, HC for humorous conversation, HD for humorous description). When you come across a good example of Durrell's humour in the book, mark the passage lightly in the margin with the appropriate letters of your code, and make a brief note of the passage (enough to recall it to you) on the sheet, always with a page reference, to save you laborious back-tracking later.

Try not to limit yourself to one aspect only: consider not only, say, Durrell's humour, but also his skill in characterisation, the structure of the book, and so on. You want to avoid narrow specialisation; it is risky in practical terms (the question might not come up) and it is grossly unfair to the author.

Take your time over this second reading. If your first reading was to savour the book and form a tentative plan of approach, during this second reading you will discover whether your approach is the right one (sometimes a bright idea turns out to be unsatisfactory, and you find yourself unable to support your argument by reference to the text). Even more crucially, now is the time to find out whether you will enjoy developing your idea further.

When you have completed your second reading, look over your notes. The jottings under each column heading should give you material for developing your argument on the subject, and you will find it good practice to try to rewrite these jottings in brief essay form. Rephrasing your notes and arranging them to show your line of argument will help to clarify your views of the subject.

At this point you might like to check your knowledge of the text. Read through the 'Detailed summaries' above (pages 12–39) and see how much you remember of each chapter.

If time permits you should read through the book yet again. By now you should have a clear idea of the aspects that interest you and of the type of examination question you could tackle. During this third reading keep your ideas in mind and check them against the text to see if your argument holds. You may well find that you have to modify your views a little more.

Quotations

During your second and third reading be on the lookout for quotations to support your views. Although, generally speaking, it is far more difficult to memorise quotations from a prose work than from a poem or a play (the sheer volume of words is against you, and there are no rhymes or metre to aid your memory), Durrell's gift for a telling, amusing phrase will be of help to you (the mother scorpion 'scattering babies like confetti' in Chapter 9; 'toast in a melting shawl of butter' in Chapter 6; Larry sinking into the mud 'like a sort of sportsmen's Shelley' in Chapter 12).

If your chosen subject is Durrell's style or his humour, you are much more likely to use quotations to illustrate your argument than in an essay on, for instance, the structure of the book or on the role of nature in Durrell's writing.

In other words, if you are concerned with the way Durrell uses words, whether to convey an image or to make his readers laugh, then obviously examples of his method will be useful. Avoid misquoting the author; do not try to memorise too many phrases, and certainly avoid trying to learn lengthy passages by heart, as under the stress of examination conditions your memory may fail you. If you are not sure of the exact words, refer to a passage indirectly (refer to Durrell's witty description of the descent of the scorpion family on the dining-table if you cannot remember 'scattering babies like confetti', or to Larry in the mud comparing himself to the drowning poet Shelley, instead of 'like a sort of sportsmen's Shelley').

It is a part of the examination myth to believe that examiners will give higher marks to the student who offers quotations. Marks will be given for quotations used in the right place to illustrate or strengthen an argument, not for quotations dragged in just because a student had learnt them by heart and cannot bear to waste them.

Preparing for the examination

The systematic reading sketched out above in the section on 'Studying the text', plus the hints on 'Quotations' should be sufficient to prepare you for an examination. In addition, you might find it useful both as practice and as reassurance to test yourself in examination conditions.

First check how many questions you will be expected to answer, and how much time you will have. Work out the time allocated to each question, but remember to give yourself extra time to read over your answers. Now choose a question from the list below (start timing yourself *before* you decide on the question, as you will not be given extra time for deciding during the examination). Work without reference to the text.

Once you have decided which question you will answer, jot down your line of approach, or your arguments for and against. (Remember that you do not have to come down on one side of the argument: you can offer reasons both for and against, and leave the conclusion open.) Now you can start writing.

First, a brief introductory outline: the subject of the question and the way in which you propose to deal with it.

Second, your argument, set out point by point, with references to the text (by quotation or by referring to a particular scene or person). Beware of simply paraphrasing the book: any references must be relevant to your argument, and should be brief.

Third, a summing up which gathers together the points made in the second part and offers a conclusion (which may of course be an open one).

While you are writing, keep referring back to the actual wording of the question, to make sure that your answer has not strayed from the point. When you have finished read through your answer carefully, looking out for any spelling errors and words missed out when writing under pressure.

It is advisable to repeat the exercise, selecting a question which deals with a different aspect of the book and demands a different approach, to give you wider experience in tackling questions.

Specimen questions

(1) 'Gerald Durrell's humour is repetitive and monotonous.' Do you agree?
(2) *My Family and Other Animals*: what does the title tell you about the book?
(3) Discuss Durrell's use of dialogue.
(4) 'A gentle, enthusiastic and understanding Noah'. Is this a good description of Mrs Durrell?
(5) Could *My Family and Other Animals* have been written by someone not interested in natural history?
(6) To what extent can *My Family and Other Animals* be regarded as a work of fiction?
(7) Do you think that Gerry's animals should have been included in any discussion of the characters in the book?
(8) Compare George and Kralefsky in their rôles as Gerry's tutors.
(9) Discuss the use of chronological order in the structure of the book.
(10) Comment on Durrell's use of simile and metaphor in his descriptive passages.

Specimen answers

(2) *My Family and Other Animals*: what does the title tell you about the book?

Surely every author regards the choosing of the right title for his book as a serious business. Quite apart from the practical aspect—an interesting, intriguing title will draw potential readers quite as much as an attractive cover picture—the title of a book is a declaration of intent on the part of its author, a summing up of the nature and purpose of the book.

Obviously Gerald Durrell chose the title *My Family and Other Animals* with great care. The first thing the title tells us is that it is a funny book, meant to entertain the readers. The title contains a hidden joke at the expense of Durrell's noisy, unruly family. After all, 'Other Animals' implies clearly that Durrell's family is to be counted among the animals in the book, whether for the untidy, undisciplined way it behaves, or for its simple, natural behaviour.

On a more serious level, however, we might say that the title is a declaration of equality between men and animals. What may have started as a hidden joke can be seen as a hidden statement of a world view which goes right back to St Francis of Assisi, who spoke of his brother wolf, and which has gained currency particularly in the last few decades with the growth of the ecology movement. Man's right to use and abuse other creatures, based on the anthropocentric view of the universe, is being questioned, and the rights of animals are being asserted, albeit by people speaking on their behalf. (In Britain, for instance, there now exists an Animal Liberation Front, a society which occasionally hits the newspaper headlines because of its violent protests against vivisection of animals for purposes of medical research for the benefit of humanity.)

In the book the boy Gerry certainly sees people and animals in much the same light. He tells us, for instance, that he and his dog Roger laid bets as to which of two fighting male tortoises would win the battle, and that Roger usually lost, having backed a loser. Here the boy and dog are equals, engaged in a human activity. In the description of the battle between the gecko Geronimo and the mantid Cicely not only are both creatures given human names but their activities are described in human terms. Cicely lands on the wall of Gerry's bedroom and looks round 'with an air of grim interest, like an angular spinster in an art gallery', while the gecko is taken aback by her insolence in daring to settle on his territory, and decides to teach the 'impertinent insect' a lesson. By assuming that the gecko and the mantid react to events as people would, Gerry shows that to him there is no difference between them and humans. This may be taking the title too seriously, but the suggestion is there.

On another level again the title is a reminder of the way in which the nature of the book changed while Durrell was writing it. In the introductory 'Speech for the Defence' he tells us that he had in mind 'a mildly nostalgic account of the natural history' of the island of Corfu, but that he made the mistake of bringing in his family who at once took over and elbowed out the animals. The family, the title might be saying, now comes first and the animals take second place.

The title may be interpreted in several ways, but the one characteristic all these interpretations have in common is an awareness of words and their meanings, and a skill in using them to amuse and perhaps to instruct as well.

---

(9) Discuss the use of chronological order in the structure of the book.

In a book which deals with the natural history of a defined area (which had been Gerald Durrell's original purpose before he succumbed to the temptation to write instead about his eccentric, amusing family) the author is presented with a choice of two ways of approach.

He can follow the seasonal changes as reflected in the fauna and flora of the area as a whole, or he can take one small area at a time—the mountains, say, the seaside or river banks, the meadows or the woodlands—and describe it in detail, noting any seasonal changes as necessary.

Gerald Durrell chose for his book a combination of these two approaches. As a glance at the contents page will show, the book is divided into three main sections, each dealing with events, people and animals linked with the house in which the Durrells were then living. As they moved first to a small pink house, then to a yellow villa large enough to accommodate all the people Larry had invited to come and stay, and finally to a small white house, chosen so that they could truthfully declare to the dreaded Great-aunt Hermione that their house is too small for visitors, the changes of location follow each other in a chronological order.

In addition a second chronological order imposes itself on the narrative. This is the seasonal round of spring, summer, autumn and winter. It is spring when the Durrells come to Corfu and settle in the pink villa. When summer approaches, bringing numerous visitors, they move to the yellow villa where they remain for the autumn and winter as well. In the spring Great-aunt Hermione's letter arrives and they move again, to the white villa.

Such a brief summary of seasonal chronology is misleading, however. *My Family and Other Animals* is an account of five years in Corfu, and while no indication is given of the length of stay in each house, the nostalgic references to quickly established annual treats and pleasures—such as the visits to the lily fields by Lake Antiniotissa, the autumnal duck shoots and snipe shoots so enjoyed by Leslie, the dove shooting in the spring, the springtime courtship rituals of the tortoises—hint at the passing of years. The order of events, therefore, is chronological inasmuch as the three moves follow one another, but the seasonal changes and the enjoyments which they bring, whilst recorded within a framework of roughly one year, cover the entire period of the Durrells' stay in Corfu.

This device enables the author to convey a sense of tranquil continuity which is one of the book's most attractive features. The Durrells' stay in Corfu was short enough to make this possible: no great changes took place during this period apart from the changes which the seasons of the year bring. These changes, observed and recorded by the author with such evident delight, form the background for human activities, fixed firmly in the seasonal round.

We might say that the book is constructed on a double chronological order. First, the sequence of the three moves, which gives the book its division into three parts, and, second, the chronology of the four seasons. These are described within the three parts, but, belonging to the never ending cycle of nature, they have a chronology of their own which gives the book its sense of a peaceful continuity of assured happiness.

Though in 'The Speech for the Defence' we are told that the Durrells stayed on Corfu for five years, once the story of their life on the island starts, the author ceases to concern himself with dates. It would not be possible to work out really how long the family stayed in each of the three villas, nor is it desirable to do so. The reader's enjoyment lies precisely in the savouring of recurring seasonal pleasures which are timeless.

Part 5

Suggestions for further reading

The text

DURRELL, GERALD: *My Family and Other Animals*, Penguin Books, Harmondsworth, 1969. This paperback edition is the only edition easily obtainable at the present time.

Other works by Gerald Durrell

The list of Gerald Durrell's published books is long, but not all of them are still available today. The following are all in print and offer a representative selection:

DURRELL, GERALD: *The Bafut Beagles*, Penguin Books, Harmondsworth, 1958.
——— : *Birds, Beasts and Relatives*, Penguin Books, Harmondsworth, 1977.
——— : *Menagerie Manor*, Penguin Books, Harmondsworth, 1975.
——— : *The Overloaded Ark*, Faber Paperbacks, London, 1987.
——— : *The Whispering Land*, Penguin Books, Harmondsworth, 1975.
——— : *A Zoo in My Luggage*, Penguin Books, Harmondsworth, 1976.

Background reading

DURRELL, LAWRENCE: *Prospero's Cell*, new edn, Faber, London, 1975. Paperback edition, Faber, London, 1974. Very different from *My Family and Other Animals*, and thus offers an interesting comparison.

The author of these notes

HANA SAMBROOK was educated at the Charles University in Prague and at the University of Edinburgh. She worked as an editor in educational publishing and was for some years on the staff of the Edinburgh University Library. Now a freelance editor in London, she is the author of York Notes on *The Tenant of Wildfell Hall*, *Lark Rise to Candleford*, and *Victory*.

York Notes: list of titles

CHINUA ACHEBE
A Man of the People
Arrow of God
Things Fall Apart
EDWARD ALBEE
Who's Afraid of Virginia Woolf?
ELECHI AMADI
The Concubine
ANONYMOUS
Beowulf
Everyman
AYI KWEI ARMAH
The Beautyful Ones Are Not Yet Born
W. H. AUDEN
Selected Poems
JANE AUSTEN
Emma
Mansfield Park
Northanger Abbey
Persuasion
Pride and Prejudice
Sense and Sensibility
HONORÉ DE BALZAC
Le Père Goriot
SAMUEL BECKETT
Waiting for Godot
SAUL BELLOW
Henderson, The Rain King
ARNOLD BENNETT
Anna of the Five Towns
The Card
WILLIAM BLAKE
Songs of Innocence, Songs of Experience
ROBERT BOLT
A Man For All Seasons
HAROLD BRIGHOUSE
Hobson's Choice
ANNE BRONTË
The Tenant of Wildfell Hall
CHARLOTTE BRONTË
Jane Eyre
EMILY BRONTË
Wuthering Heights
ROBERT BROWNING
Men and Women
JOHN BUCHAN
The Thirty-Nine Steps
JOHN BUNYAN
The Pilgrim's Progress
BYRON
Selected Poems
ALBERT CAMUS
L'Etranger (The Outsider)
GEOFFREY CHAUCER
Prologue to the Canterbury Tales
The Clerk's Tale
The Franklin's Tale
The Knight's Tale
The Merchant's Tale
The Miller's Tale
The Nun's Priest's Tale
The Pardoner's Tale
The Wife of Bath's Tale
Troilus and Criseyde
ANTON CHEKOV
The Cherry Orchard
SAMUEL TAYLOR COLERIDGE
Selected Poems
WILKIE COLLINS
The Moonstone
SIR ARTHUR CONAN DOYLE
The Hound of the Baskervilles
WILLIAM CONGREVE
The Way of the World
JOSEPH CONRAD
Heart of Darkness
Lord Jim
Nostromo
The Secret Agent
Victory
Youth and *Typhoon*
STEPHEN CRANE
The Red Badge of Courage
BRUCE DAWE
Selected Poems
WALTER DE LA MARE
Selected Poems
DANIEL DEFOE
A Journal of the Plague Year
Moll Flanders
Robinson Crusoe
CHARLES DICKENS
A Tale of Two Cities
Bleak House
David Copperfield
Dombey and Son
Great Expectations
Hard Times
Little Dorrit
Oliver Twist
Our Mutual Friend
The Pickwick Papers
EMILY DICKINSON
Selected Poems
JOHN DONNE
Selected Poems
JOHN DRYDEN
Selected Poems
GERALD DURRELL
My Family and Other Animals
GEORGE ELIOT
Adam Bede
Middlemarch
Silas Marner
The Mill on the Floss
T. S. ELIOT
Four Quartets
Murder in the Cathedral
Selected Poems
The Cocktail Party
The Waste Land
J. G. FARRELL
The Siege of Krishnapur
GEORGE FARQUHAR
The Beaux Stratagem
WILLIAM FAULKNER
Absalom, Absalom!
The Sound and the Fury
HENRY FIELDING
Joseph Andrews
Tom Jones
F. SCOTT FITZGERALD
Tender is the Night
The Great Gatsby

List of titles

GUSTAVE FLAUBERT
Madame Bovary
E. M. FORSTER
A Passage to India
Howards End
JOHN FOWLES
The French Lieutenant's Woman
ATHOL FUGARD
Selected Plays
JOHN GALSWORTHY
Strife
MRS GASKELL
North and South
WILLIAM GOLDING
Lord of the Flies
The Spire
OLIVER GOLDSMITH
She Stoops to Conquer
The Vicar of Wakefield
ROBERT GRAVES
Goodbye to All That
GRAHAM GREENE
Brighton Rock
The Heart of the Matter
The Power and the Glory
WILLIS HALL
The Long and the Short and the Tall
THOMAS HARDY
Far from the Madding Crowd
Jude the Obscure
Selected Poems
Tess of the D'Urbervilles
The Mayor of Casterbridge
The Return of the Native
The Trumpet Major
The Woodlanders
Under the Greenwood Tree
L. P. HARTLEY
The Go-Between
The Shrimp and the Anemone
NATHANIEL HAWTHORNE
The Scarlet Letter
SEAMUS HEANEY
Selected Poems
JOSEPH HELLER
Catch-22
ERNEST HEMINGWAY
A Farewell to Arms
For Whom the Bell Tolls
The Old Man and the Sea
GEORGE HERBERT
Selected Poems
HERMANN HESSE
Steppenwolf
BARRY HINES
Kes
HOMER
The Iliad
The Odyssey
ANTHONY HOPE
The Prisoner of Zenda
GERARD MANLEY HOPKINS
Selected Poems
WILLIAM DEAN HOWELLS
The Rise of Silas Lapham
RICHARD HUGHES
A High Wind in Jamaica
TED HUGHES
Selected Poems
THOMAS HUGHES
Tom Brown's Schooldays

ALDOUS HUXLEY
Brave New World
HENRIK IBSEN
A Doll's House
Ghosts
HENRY JAMES
Daisy Miller
The Ambassadors
The Europeans
The Portrait of a Lady
The Turn of the Screw
Washington Square
SAMUEL JOHNSON
Rasselas
BEN JONSON
The Alchemist
Volpone
JAMES JOYCE
A Portrait of the Artist as a Young Man
Dubliners
JOHN KEATS
Selected Poems
RUDYARD KIPLING
Kim
D. H. LAWRENCE
Sons and Lovers
The Rainbow
Women in Love
CAMARA LAYE
L'Enfant Noir
HARPER LEE
To Kill a Mocking-Bird
LAURIE LEE
Cider with Rosie
THOMAS MANN
Tonio Kröger
CHRISTOPHER MARLOWE
Doctor Faustus
ANDREW MARVELL
Selected Poems
W. SOMERSET MAUGHAM
Selected Short Stories
GAVIN MAXWELL
Ring of Bright Water
J. MEADE FALKNER
Moonfleet
HERMAN MELVILLE
Billy Budd
Moby Dick
THOMAS MIDDLETON
Women Beware Women
THOMAS MIDDLETON and WILLIAM ROWLEY
The Changeling
ARTHUR MILLER
A View from the Bridge
Death of a Salesman
The Crucible
JOHN MILTON
Paradise Lost I & II
Paradise Lost IV & IX
Selected Poems
V. S. NAIPAUL
A House for Mr Biswas
ROBERT O'BRIEN
Z for Zachariah
SEAN O'CASEY
Juno and the Paycock
GABRIEL OKARA
The Voice
EUGENE O'NEILL
Mourning Becomes Electra

List of titles

GEORGE ORWELL
Animal Farm
Nineteen Eighty-four

JOHN OSBORNE
Look Back in Anger

WILFRED OWEN
Selected Poems

ALAN PATON
Cry, The Beloved Country

THOMAS LOVE PEACOCK
Nightmare Abbey and *Crotchet Castle*

HAROLD PINTER
The Caretaker

PLATO
The Republic

ALEXANDER POPE
Selected Poems

J. B. PRIESTLEY
An Inspector Calls

THOMAS PYNCHON
The Crying of Lot 49

SIR WALTER SCOTT
Ivanhoe
Quentin Durward
The Heart of Midlothian
Waverley

PETER SHAFFER
The Royal Hunt of the Sun

WILLIAM SHAKESPEARE
A Midsummer Night's Dream
Antony and Cleopatra
As You Like It
Coriolanus
Cymbeline
Hamlet
Henry IV Part I
Henry IV Part II
Henry V
Julius Caesar
King Lear
Love's Labour's Lost
Macbeth
Measure for Measure
Much Ado About Nothing
Othello
Richard II
Richard III
Romeo and Juliet
Sonnets
The Merchant of Venice
The Taming of the Shrew
The Tempest
The Winter's Tale
Troilus and Cressida
Twelfth Night

GEORGE BERNARD SHAW
Androcles and the Lion
Arms and the Man
Caesar and Cleopatra
Candida
Major Barbara
Pygmalion
Saint Joan
The Devil's Disciple

MARY SHELLEY
Frankenstein

PERCY BYSSHE SHELLEY
Selected Poems

RICHARD BRINSLEY SHERIDAN
The School for Scandal
The Rivals

R. C. SHERRIFF
Journey's End

WOLE SOYINKA
The Road
Three Short Plays

EDMUND SPENSER
The Faerie Queene (Book I)

JOHN STEINBECK
Of Mice and Men
The Grapes of Wrath
The Pearl

LAURENCE STERNE
A Sentimental Journey
Tristram Shandy

ROBERT LOUIS STEVENSON
Kidnapped
Treasure Island
Dr Jekyll and Mr Hyde

TOM STOPPARD
Professional Foul
Rosencrantz and Guildenstern are Dead

JONATHAN SWIFT
Gulliver's Travels

JOHN MILLINGTON SYNGE
The Playboy of the Western World

TENNYSON
Selected Poems

W. M. THACKERAY
Vanity Fair

DYLAN THOMAS
Under Milk Wood

EDWARD THOMAS
Selected Poems

FLORA THOMPSON
Lark Rise to Candleford

J. R. R. TOLKIEN
The Hobbit
The Lord of the Rings

ANTHONY TROLLOPE
Barchester Towers

MARK TWAIN
Huckleberry Finn
Tom Sawyer

JOHN VANBRUGH
The Relapse

VIRGIL
The Aeneid

VOLTAIRE
Candide

KEITH WATERHOUSE
Billy Liar

EVELYN WAUGH
Decline and Fall

JOHN WEBSTER
The Duchess of Malfi
The White Devil

H. G. WELLS
The History of Mr Polly
The Invisible Man
The War of the Worlds

OSCAR WILDE
The Importance of Being Earnest

THORNTON WILDER
Our Town

TENNESSEE WILLIAMS
The Glass Menagerie

VIRGINIA WOOLF
Mrs Dalloway
To the Lighthouse

WILLIAM WORDSWORTH
Selected Poems

WILLIAM WYCHERLEY
The Country Wife

W. B. YEATS
Selected Poems